THE HOOP AND THE HARM

JAWARA PEDICAN

James Lorimer and Company Ltd., Publishers
Toronto

James Lorimer & Company Ltd., Publishers acknowledges funding support from the Ontario Arts Council (OAC), an agency of the Government of Ontario. We acknowledge the support of the Canada Council for the Arts, which last year invested $153 million to bring the arts to Canadians throughout the country. This project has been made possible in part by the Government of Canada and with the support of Ontario Creates.

Cover design: Tyler Cleroux
Cover image: Shutterstock

Library and Archives Canada Cataloguing in Publication

Title: The hoop and the harm / Jawara Pedican.
Names: Pedican, Jawara, author.
Identifiers: Canadiana 20220485054 | ISBN 9781459417229 (hardcover) | ISBN 9781459417151 (softcover) | ISBN 9781459417472 (epub)
Subjects: LCGFT: Novels.
Classification: LCC PS8631.E392 H66 2023 | DDC C813/.6—dc23

Published by:
James Lorimer & Company Ltd., Publishers
117 Peter Street, Suite 304
Toronto, ON, Canada
M5V 0M3
www.lorimer.ca

Distributed in Canada by:
Formac Lorimer Books
5502 Atlantic Street
Halifax, NS, Canada
B3H 1G4
www.formaclorimerbooks.ca

Distributed in the US by:
Lerner Publisher Services
241 1st Ave. N.
Minneapolis, MN, USA
55401
www.lernerbooks.com

Printed and bound in Canada.
Manufactured by Friesens Corporation in Altona, Manitoba, Canada in February 2023.
Job #294593

Dad, this is for you. With love.

PROLOGUE

To You:

I'd be grateful if you ever read this. Because I'm sorry. Sorry for what happened to you. Sorry for what happened to us. Sorry for it all. I just hope one day you come to believe, as I do, that it's just better this way. For everyone.

It wasn't long before I knew you were special.

I was proud of you then, and I still am to this day. I kept an eye on you from afar and listened closely to the chatter around your name — the praise and the slander, all along. I knew what you went through and exactly how you felt, not because I'm familiar with your struggles — because I'm not — but because I know you. A zillion times better than you think I do, and quite possibly more than you'd recognize yourself in any mirror.

I've seen you in your brightest moments, but also within that place — that deep, ugly, dark place where doubt filled your heart. I knew when you felt mighty and thought you had it all figured out; but also when your vision was clouded by fear, when having faith in your own self seemed impossible. Like I said, man: I know you. Inside and out. Flesh and blood. Thoughts and feelings. Your hurt, your bliss, and everything that lies in between — I've felt it all. Through you. With you. Always.

Until that one time, some months ago.

You'd been in pain before, but never like that. For once in my life, I couldn't imagine what you were battling.

Moments before then, I saw this twinkle in your eyes despite your trying past, despite the bits of hope you'd lost, despite the times you'd felt like giving up. You were thriving. Happy. With a heart that was full and a soul serene. You found yourself again.

Though right then and there, in an instant, everything took a turn for the worse. You were just lying there, all agonized, not too far from me. It seemed like you were quick to forget the bliss that came and left so cruelly.

You were broken. Again. And I couldn't take it any longer, seeing you there like that.

So, I had to go.

And I can't begin to think of the defeat you've felt since then. I've spent hours — if not, days — trying to justify my leaving. I have my reasons, but hey, maybe you wouldn't wanna see me anyway. Maybe I'm the reason you need time for healing to begin with. Maybe we're like this because of all that pressure I put on you. Or maybe, just maybe, it's because I gave you reasons to feel afraid of failing, or wary of falling into that deep, ugly, dark place where you scorn yourself for achieving less than what you'd set out to accomplish.

I thought you would've despised knowing that I saw you at your lowest, so I couldn't stay. Yeah, I'll wrap my head around that excuse.

I should've been there, though. And I know it. So, if you're still reading this, I can only hope you'll someday forgive me.

Because I apologize…

I apologize if I ever gave the impression that you were anything less than gifted. Because you were. No — you are.

I apologize if, because of me, you now lead a life lived the wrong way.

A life of caution.

A life of safe, dull, uneventful days.

A life that avoids risks or moments that call for the utmost courage in yourself.

A life that shies from adversity and challenges.

A life riddled with fear.

And I apologize, I so deeply apologize, if I'm the reason you ever find yourself hesitant when the world needs you certain. Bashful when the world needs you bold and proud.

Afraid when the world needs you brave.

Because the world needs the best you that you can be. So, take your shot.

Take care of yourself, too.

Goodbye.

CHAPTER 1

PERCHED ON PIERCING THORNS

Breathe. Don't think. Just breathe. "In through your nose, out through your mouth," as they say. Relax. Close your eyes, slowly, calmly. Block out all the frantic action. Let those tense, shallow breaths effortlessly seep out of your lungs. Remove yourself from the worries, the pressure.

Gather your racing thoughts. Envision *you.* Not the *current* you in this trying time of angst, but the *ideal* you, the *best-version-of-yourself* you—thriving in whatever you do and loving every blink of it, flourishing in your own perfect world.

Now, take a moment to imagine how different life could be if you practiced mindfulness during tough times — y'know, meditation or self-affirmations or what have you. What might that feel like? Would you be more successful? Wiser? Happier? Where would you be? Perhaps in a drastically different position?

Well, don't invest too much thought in the *what-ifs*, because if you could rewind back to any single moment when you should have been calm or clear-headed, instead of caught in your worries and fears, then your life could've spun into infinite outcomes! But since you have only a moment (*remember*?), don't you dare think too deeply.

Just breathe. *Breathe.* Yeah, I'll repeat it: *breeeathe.* You can get lost in your imagination for as long as you choose, but at some point — typically sooner than you wanted — you'll reopen your eyes and take on the challenges that the world has set out for you. Just inhale slowly, then exhale even slower.

And listen. Breathe and listen.

Listen closely. Because there's a stress-sweating, panicked someone crouching in front of you, just inches away, yelling at the top of his lungs. He's got something to say, and by the frenzied look on his face, it's gotta be important.

"We've dug ourselves outta quite some hole, guys!" he shouts. "Time's against us, but now's our last chance to pull through!" Here we are, among the deafening roars from the home crowd. We're exhausted, breathless, peering into the X's and O's on his smeary clipboard.

This is our final timeout.

"We're gonna switch into our zone trap just this one

play. They're expecting man-to-man, so this'll force their audible. Look, we need one solid possession of defense! Box out, crash the glass and get into our transition game. Early! If there's a scramble, get into a quick play call. But remember..." Coach Maythorn says, pointing at the scoreboard. "We don't have much time!"

"One stop, one bucket!" a hoarse Louis hollers, panting for deep breaths. "That's all we need, fellas!"

The first timeout horn sounds.

"Coach!" the referee firmly interrupts. "We need your guys on the floor."

"We're coming!" Maythorn barks, before regaining our attention. "Listen, we've got no timeouts left! Solid defense, then we need the ball back. If you get a good look, don't hesitate! Be ready to shoot it!" About eleven seconds remain, but the shot clock has Carleton hard-pressed to shoot within only five.

"We got this!" roars a cheerful voice within the huddle, followed by several hands and fists reaching aloft and stacking upon one another.

"Lotta time left, boys!"

"Make a play!"

"Bring it home!"

"And no fouls!" Maythorn bellows. His voice drowns in the crowd's noise just before our closing five disperse onto the court.

Down by two. This is our final go. Ready as ever.

The ball gets handed to Carleton's forward, and I'm counting each time the ref swings his arm during the inbound. *One one thousand ... two one thousand ... three one thousand ... four...*

The hurried inbounder flings an ill-advised pass to avoid a costly five-second call. Even so, Louis, with his freakish near-seven-foot wingspan, manages to get a fingertip on the ball, deflecting it into Carleton's backcourt and disrupting their entire scheme to get a clean shot off. The shot clock winds down as the crowd shouts, "*Three*! *Two*! *One*!"

Carleton's All-Star guard hoists up a prayer against the suffocating defense we pledged to Maythorn. The shot misfires off the back of the rim, causing a scuffle under the basket where both teams wrestle for the rebound.

She spills toward the baseline, but I hustle to corral Her before surveying the floor and dribbling swiftly up the court. Four seconds left. I scoop Her behind my back, evading a would-be double-team at the centre line.

Three seconds.

"Right here!" I hear to my left. "Find me, I'm open!" to my right. I weave through the defense, feinting one direction to attack the other with the destiny of our season unfolding.

Carleton's defense is air-tight, but it's my own self-doubt slowing me down. In a blink, I envision the times I'd spent in empty gyms fantasizing about last-second shots like these. If there's any time to be unshakably confident of something, it's gotta be right here, right now! *Breathe*, I tell myself, feeling the shrieks from the crowd. This game's in the palm of my hands, just like the leather skin and round seams of the ball itself.

Two precious seconds remain.

Within the clock's final ticks, I take one last bounce before stopping on a dime, inches behind the arc. "Shoot it!" screams Maythorn. I fight past my hand-checking, jersey-tugging defender. He doesn't hinder my poise — not even in the slightest. Sweat trickles down my cheeks. Doubt or no doubt, this game's mine to win.

Final second.

Over a pair of defenders and their outstretched arms, I let Her go — a fingernail from deflection. She ascends like a work of art. I watch Her float in what seems like slow motion. She kisses the backboard before circling around the basket, slowly, as though She's too wary to enter.

Suddenly, the buzzer sounds…

* * *

"Coach!" the referee intervenes once more, urging our five to take to the floor after the second timeout horn.

Ah, shucks. Remember that spiel about not thinking too deeply into the whole "mindfulness" thing? Yeah, *guilty*. But I can't blame myself for daydreaming at a time like this. After all, this is what I've been waiting for since I was a scrawny little youngster ... I just never envisioned living out this moment from the bench.

"Shut it! I heard you the first six times," Maythorn barks at the rightfully impatient ref. "This is our season, guys. Every set of lines you've run this year. Every early-morning practice you've woken up for. Your blood, your sweat, your pain...." He glances at the looks on our faces, ensuring we seem determined, focused, solemn. "*Everything* was paid at the cost of what's at stake. Rise to the occasion!"

"This is it!" adds Elvin, supporting Maythorn's rally. Everyone's fired up. In a conference quarterfinal, from a late seventeen-point deficit, to trailing by a single basket before the game's final play, how couldn't you be? I'm baffled by such a question.

It's mind-boggling — infuriating, even — that the answer is somehow beyond me.

What's nearby, though, is an open spot along the bench near the other freshmen, away but not too far from the coaches so that I won't have my ears rung off for tuning out of the game. I despise submitting to this, but I can't say I'm surprised. I'll have to let this game unfold without me.

* * *

My head rests against the chilled window; my cheek is clammy and numb. Into the never-ending carpet of barren land, we ride. Many are fast asleep, probably already fantasizing about their glories of next season. But oh, not me. I'm overwhelmed and confused and tormented by the conflict between disappointment and satisfaction. Regret, yet relief. It keeps me wide awake as the team bus sweeps along the vacant freeway. I wonder how this reality came about. I could have done more. I *should* have done more.

"Is it my fault?"

"Say what?" Elvin responds, awoken by my voice. He removes his headphones, although I'm close enough to notice his music is either playing very faintly or not at all. I forgot I wasn't alone in my row.

"Nothing. My bad."

"Aight, man." He wraps his headphones across his face and drags them onto his ears, one side at a time.

A silence plagues the ride in the few hours after our loss. All I can hear is the subtle ticking of the indicator when the driver changes lanes, and the drone-like undertone of the bus's raspy engine. No one is speaking. Not a whisper. Not a mutter.

Until, of course, someone does: "Final game of the season and all I had was four points. Six turnovers, too. Damnit, man," whines Louis, I assume. I remember him having an awful game. I wonder if he's seeking our pity or simply poking a needle into this bubble of unbearable silence.

"Don't worry, bro. You scored with that sweet Tinder match from last night, though! Probably had a couple turnovers too, I bet!" Several heads turn; chirps and giggles arise.

"Shut up, man," Louis snickers.

That must've been Conrad. He's got a knack for lightening the mood. There's a better chance of scoring nothing but net on a full-court heave than having him turn down an attempt at levity. But we love Conrad for that, his daft and often untimely antics. Blabbering about your affairs from the night before a playoff game (a game lost, I might add), especially with a disgruntled Maythorn possibly listening from a near row ahead — yeah, this has Conrad written all over it.

He's our do-it-all, Swiss-Army-knife power forward who isn't in the starting line-up but definitely finds his way into the rotation because of his lockdown, low-post defense. Conrad oozes upside, and having just concluded a breakout season as the team's leader in rebounds, steals, and nearly atop the team in scoring, I suppose he lets his game excuse him from the nonsense he blurts. Had he been glued to the bench all season long, his clowning wouldn't fly with anyone on this bus.

I look for Maythorn and anticipate his reaction. "C'mon, we just lost, guys!" he shouts, turning his head with a glare.

Maythorn and I share a mutual frustration. We just let a winnable playoff game slip away like sand seeping through a tightly clenched fist. And the chatter of the team — Louis's whereabouts with some shallow swipe-right the night before the most important game of his career.

In an instant, I can feel the mood take a one-eighty. It seems like no one's troubled about the loss anymore, as though droopy postures and sulking faces were just a temporary phase. We were a basket away from a possible trip to Nationals, yet everyone seems so content now. And all it took was some silly locker room gossip.

I, like Maythorn, would have preferred silence on the ride back home. Just like how it was minutes ago. How it should be after a tough, season-ending loss. So this snide "it's just a game" attitude going around is not helping me.

But then again, I'm reminded of my own hypocrisy.

Of course I wanted us to win, but it's not like I was able to snap my fingers or take a swig from "Michael's Secret Stuff" and magically become all mighty and fearless for a clutch final play. No, I don't play for the Tune Squad of '96, and no, it doesn't work that way, either. So, despite the voice in my head telling me I should've fought to be out there, I had no business playing in the heat of crunch time, anyway.

And I hate to admit it.

* * *

I'm wakened by something grazing my neck, tapping to the bounce of the bus as it speeds along the 401. I turn my head to find it's someone's foot covered in a smelly, dark green sock with a silver flash across the ankle. It's Elvin's. He's out cold with his feet on my headrest, lying along the seats adjacent to mine. And I can't blame him. Road trips are super uncomfortable to sit through, and it's tough getting some shuteye while confined at the hips and knees for several hours — especially if you're six-foot-nine, like he is. Even still, his reeky feet dangling in my face leave me no choice but to shove them away. He wakes abruptly.

"Ah! My bad, big dog."

"It's all good, man."

He yawns. "Yo, Duke."

"What's up?"

"You want the last one?" Elvin snags the remains of the team's post-game meal, a lone Hawaiian slice shuffling from one end of the box to the other as the bus turns sharply.

I glance at it, then at him. "Nah. Thanks, though." Usually, I find an appetite to munch on something, even cold, brittle pizza. But not this time.

This time's different. I played an awful game; it was unsettling to think about, not only for my stomach. As poor of an outing Louis had, I'd cringe checking the spread for my stats. See, at least Louis contributed.

He still made winning plays to help us cut down the deficit. He drew a pair of offensive fouls late in the third quarter. He was vocal. He snatched maybe six or seven rebounds and moved the ball so others could score. He didn't score a bunch of his own, but he helped the team like he usually does.

As for me, I played timid. Tentative. Afraid to make a decisive play or get a couple shots off. Everyone knew I was having a lousy game — my teammates, Carleton's squad, the fans hollering from the stands. They could sense my jitters, the stiffness in my moves. It was like *DO NOT PASS TO ME* was stitched boldly on the back of my uniform above my jersey number, instead of my last name. I mean, it's upsetting thinking that my teammates no longer believe in me. Yet what's worse is realizing my wrong in playing the victim, my wrong in fretting about what others believe I can or can't do when it's apparent that the little belief in *myself* is the problem.

"On second thought," I eventually reply, glancing again at the leftover pizza, "nah, never mind. I'm straight."

"Cool," replies Elvin. "Offer's still on the table."

"Seat."

"Huh?"

"The offer. You mean it's on the seat. Y'know, beside you?" I suggest, giggling subtly, hoping a jab at his misused figure of speech will lighten us up. He raises an eyebrow instead. It was pathetic, snarky humour, Elv. I know.

"Yeah," he hisses, "whatever, Duke."

Ah, *Duke*. I hear a teasing echo in my head and find myself smirking, slightly annoyed but light-hearted nonetheless. It's not like Elvin, or Maythorn, or anyone else in these rows couldn't pronounce my name — Udoka — because they all can, and perhaps I can't even blame them for the "*Duke*" thing, since I've been too meek to oppose it, but there's a history behind the nicknames I've been given.

When I was little, maybe four or five years old, my mum used to enunciate each of my name's three syllables to strangers because I was too shy to assert myself on my own. "*Oo-doh-kuh.* See, it's easy! Say it! *Oo-doh-kuh. Udoka*!" she'd exclaim to them, whether they were distant relatives or whoever I'd meet for the first time. "No, it's not '*You,*' it's '*Oo*!'" I'd hide behind her, wrapping myself around her leg, feeling embarrassed and unwilling to cause a scene or make a big deal about a grown-up butchering my name — as if their inability to say it properly was inconvenient to *them* and not me. Maybe I was too young to realize those battles should've been mine to fight.

As I aged, I would groan whenever people confused me with *Utica,* the small city in the state of New York. Ideally, I would have fired back with something like, "Say it right or don't even call for me, period!" That is, if the prideful and assertive and no-bullshit-taking version of me trapped inside my mind and screaming to come out would ever get a chance to take over. But nope, it never broke the lock.

See, where I'm from — my humble grounds in the city's west end, Jane and St. Clair, to be specific — they call me *Yoosie* because of my initials: *U.C.*, as in Udoka Clendon. It makes me think of my old middle school teachers when I'd ask if I could go to the washroom right after recess. They'd say, "Can you? Can you get up and go relieve yourself? You seem capable. But *may* you? *May* you go right before this lesson begins?" Their answer was often "no."

So, likewise, the hidden, no-bullshit-taking version of me should've been saying, "Can you call me *Yoosie*? Sure, it's doable. Now, *may* you call me by whatever you choose, simply because it's easier for you? Nuh-uh! Ain't gonna happen!" I'd envision this "me" kissing his teeth and storming off from the scene.

But eventually, the actual version of me — the one that's unfortunately not as brash or unapologetically intolerant to bullshit as it needs to be — came to ignore the tag *Yoosie* instead of opposing it. Then came acceptance. Then, soon enough, I ran with *Yoosie* and didn't respond to anything else — until now.

So, to the team, I am Duke. Which isn't the worst deal, because I like that I was given a nickname — since, on any team, it represents a fondness, a bond between you and your crew. I mean, yeah, this whole "*Duke*" thing is still foreign to me — especially since having been a die-hard fan and past hopeful of donning the Carolina Blue when I was younger — but it's not all so bad because the team embraces me all the same.

* * *

The sun rises behind a forest of skyscrapers on the downtown horizon, where the CN Tower's needle pokes through the sky. We're finally a few stoplights from campus as a blade of sunlight shoots into the bus, from the front row to the rear. I've been wide awake for a while now, caught thinking about what's next for me without a clear sight in mind. It has me all tripped out. Stuffing gear into my duffle bag hasn't turned out to be the distraction I hoped for.

Because inside the bag, I find my practice jersey, reminding me of that early-morning rush to get on the court in time for training, and how quickly I'd scramble to suit up while fighting that minutes-to-6:00 a.m. lethargy that I shared with the rest of the guys. Crammed somewhere in the side compartments are my ankle braces. I think of the nagging tweaks and sprains I've sustained in the past year but more so the guys' encouraging words that had driven me to recover as soon as I could. My game shoes are jammed somewhere in here too, bringing me back to the sound of squeaks on the hardwood, the calling of my name from the scorer's table, the proud victories and the humbling defeats. The jersey, the braces, the sneakers — they're all bringing me to realize that the season is over. And that sucks, because I love these guys, man.

"You're in a hurry," says Elvin.

I shrug. I guess he's right.

The *take cares* and *best of lucks* from the seniors are nearing, and I could imagine season-ending goodbyes being tear-jerking for some of them. For guys like me, there aren't many situations more awkward than struggling to reciprocate something heartfelt for a teammate who's typically so tough on the outside. Should I get sucked into a farewell, I'll probably go with, *"Imma carry the torch for you, bro,"* then follow with a dap and a hug with my other arm, hoping not to break a straight face.

But aside from that reason, I want to hop off this bus without a peep at anyone because I fear situating myself on the seniors' end of the goodbyes too. I mean, the guys knew this was a crummy season for me, but they'd all be surprised if I told them it might be my last.

I nudge Elvin. "See you around," I tell him, shuffling past the rows while the bus comes to a halt. He nods at me, so I nod back.

* * *

My duffle bag sways back and forth as I waddle along the platform at St. Patrick Station, and I'm beginning to feel the rumble approaching the mint green tunnel. I reach into my pocket and feel for my phone, the thin button along the side that gets it vibrating once held for a beat. I notice three things from its lock screen — one, it's *6:48 a.m.* on a calm Thursday morning; two, my phone is destined to die, proving my theory that travel bus outlets are reliably unreliable; and three, this:

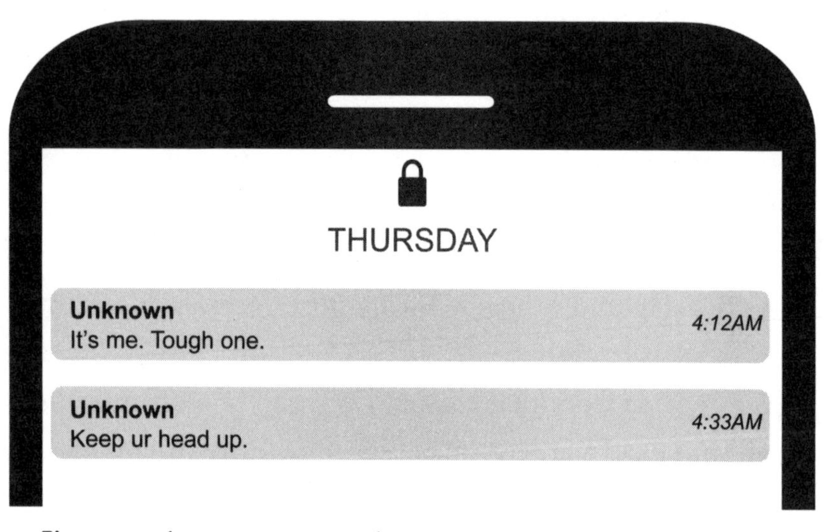

I'm caught staring at these texts as the train gusts toward me and screeches to slow down. I can only wonder who'd sent them and why at such an early hour. If it is you, though, and if this is the end of my journey, for what it's worth, I hope I made you proud.

Wherever you are.

CHAPTER 11

ANOTHER LAP

Conrad wheezes and hunches over with the weight of his body resting on his knees. His breath disappears into the chilly, peak-of-winter air.

"Why're we doing this right now, anyway?" he asks, hanging his head into his chest, staring at the crooked chalk line that runs across the clay track. He gasps for air as though he wishes the track had somehow been downsized to surround anything smaller than a football field — a tennis court, maybe. His gaze ascends from the dirt to a dozen other wheezing and hunched-over bodies, and suddenly he's reminded that he's not enduring this alone.

"For next season," says Arlen, our strength and conditioning coach. He's wearing dark green sweatpants tapered at the ankles, and a grey, long-sleeve sweatshirt with *WOLFPACK BASKETBALL* stitched across the chest. The shirt is fitted snugly, emphasizing his build and "alpha sports trainer" image.

"It's not like we run track," Conrad complains. "We're the basketball team."

"Are we the *winning* basketball team?"

Conrad winces but doesn't reply. He removes his toque and shakes the beads of sweat from his wet, spiky hair like a pup after a bath.

Arlen repeats, "Are we?"

"Nah."

"So, until then, we gotta train like one! Winning teams are prepping for tonight's semis, right now," Arlen continues, "while you're busy complaining!"

"We lost like … two days ago, man."

"Which means Carleton *won,* like, two days ago, *man*! They're exactly where we should've been." Arlen sighs. "Where we wanna be."

"All these sprints…" Conrad angles his chin to the sky, reaching for every whiff of frigid air to fill his lungs before saying another word. "They won't help us 'til next year's semis."

"You ever made it to a conference semifinal?"

Conrad gives Arlen a hostile glare.

Arlen persists. "Have you?"

"Nah."

"Come again?"

"No."

"No, *who*?"

"No, Coach."

"So, explain to me — how do you know what'll help us for the semis, or what won't, if you've never even been there?"

Arlen awaits any lame response. I wonder if Conrad will either shut his mouth or embrace his shovel and proceed digging himself deeper into the hole he's created.

Conrad mutters, "Whatever."

"What was that?"

Clearing his throat, again Conrad says, "Whatever."

"*Gentlemeeen*! *Congratulations*!" A heavy groan resonates from within the team. Nothing good can come from this. "Add on three more sprints, fellas! Two hundred meters apiece! Last five guys of each sprint'll run again!"

As though Conrad hasn't yet learned, he builds up the audacity to poke at Arlen's seething temper. "But why?"

"Make that the four hundred! Full extra lap for the bottom five."

"Great," Elvin murmurs, a patch of sweat seeping along the neck of his hoodie. He firmly brushes Conrad's shoulder as he walks by, as though to say, *Shut the hell up, already*, but the gesture is still subtle and easy and contained inside the little box of Elvin's nice-guy personality.

Louis buries his face into his sweatshirt and swipes his sleeve across his forehead, mumbling, "We'll be track stars by next week if you keep at it."

But in defense of Conrad's backtalk, we are witnessing an unprecedented version of Arlen. A sterner, pushier Arlen. An Arlen unwilling to stoop below the benchmark of discipline that he had laid out since preseason, but, through a slip of his mind, had now somehow forgotten. I guess he internalized the Carleton loss just as much as we did.

I glance at the sour faces surrounding me. Elvin's, Louis's, the freshmen's. Conrad's. They exchange looks — some with steeply raised eyebrows, others looking stunned, dumbfounded. They seem troubled by the thought that a long offseason has just begun. As for me? I can't quite describe how I think I look. Blank-faced, maybe. Or I'm probably squinting as sunrays pierce the cold blue skies. I dunno. But, regardless, I'm getting the idea that Arlen's mind, body, and spirit might've just been hijacked by a Mr. Edwin Maythorn.

* * *

Cold slush flings against my shins. Grainy, wet clay whips into my face. I realize I've been distracted from these measly fifty or so meters ahead of me. I turn my head left and right to find that I'm ahead of everyone on the team — well, all but one: Louis. Stride after stride, his runners kick more and more dirt into my path. I gotta pick up my pace.

I'm reminded of Elvin's dark green socks that he wore on the bus, with their flashy silver stitching. They're team socks. Louis is wearing a pair too. With a glimpse of them, I revisit the chilled window on which my head rested, the cold leftovers I was offered, the disappointment of losing the quarterfinals. But ultimately, I'm reminded of my once-vague contemplation of giving up this game, which is screaming at me louder than ever before. I drift into an eerie reckoning that I no longer feel one with the Wolfpack...

For once in my life, I fear a looming reality of somehow and someday having to become whole without Her.

At his top speed, Louis leans forward and darts past a kneeling Arlen, who is planted in the dirt by the finish line. Arlen peers closely into his stopwatch, a whistle dangling from his mouth. Dashing past the jagged stripe of chalk, in the blink of an eye after Louis, is when I arrive.

* * *

The afternoon snowstorm has yet to relent. Tilt your head to the sky and you'll spot not a single cloud but a blank scape instead, pale and white. I admire how the snowflakes float and take their time falling to the slushy ground. It reminds me of a snow globe, shaken and flipped right-side-up, the way the delicate ice crystals sprinkle upon everything, everywhere.

A cool breeze gusts by my cheek and reminds me

where I am, yet also where I am *not*. I wonder what the same wind against my face would feel like at this time of the year, elsewhere, had I approached this game differently; had my faith in this game remained strong around the time it began to dwindle. I picture myself dragging my feet in a comfy pair of slides, heading back to my dorm to the delight of free room and board with some long-awaited, meal-plan lasagna calling my name.

Instead, ahead of me is a wet, slippery sidewalk along University Ave. I'm treading toward St. Patrick Station with numbing hands, but I can feel my phone vibrate inside my hoodie's pouch. I'm not willing to take it out in this wind chill, but still, I catch a glimpse of the lock screen:

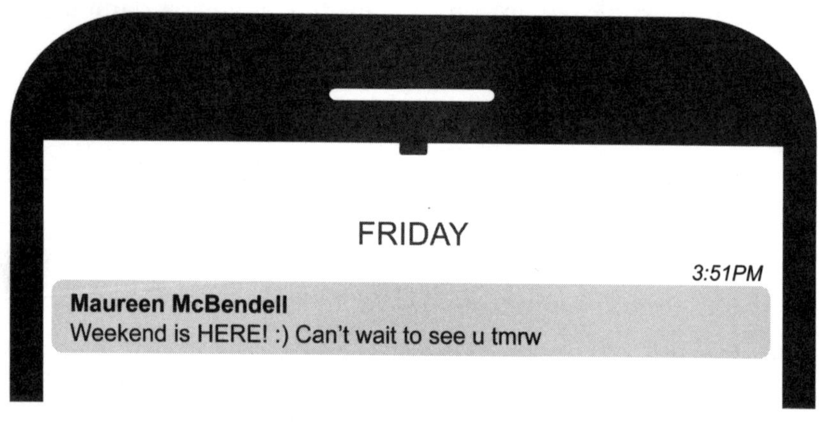

And suddenly the wind doesn't feel as chilly or my regrets as heavy.

Because I yearn to see her too.

CHAPTER III

OPENING UP

Ding! *Ding*! *Ding*! Flickering before me is a beam of sunshine intruding into the room. Bright, blurry shapes gradually take on the form of familiar objects. The speck of light from a distance turns out to be the sun reflecting off a knife from Ma's old and never used silverware set. That tall, brownish figure straight ahead is the floor lamp by the dining room table.

Ding! *Ding*! *Ding*! I flinch at the sound, toying with the thought of ignoring my phone. I already know who it is: Mo. I mean, I have no problem with her calling me this early. I'm thrilled she did, even though she always does these things, and now is no different. These things, the little things that make me truly appreciate her; the little things that make me cherish being someone's first thought the moment they take their waking breaths.

I'm wary of answering her because I know this'll be my official return to the first time, a couple summers ago. I remember it so vividly, despite how dreadful it was. The mere thought of it doesn't escape me — spewing my miseries onto Mo and relying on her to soothe the pain, feeling weak and vulnerable and without a stoic bone in my body — I don't want to return to the first time.

I jam my hand into the sofa's crevices, fishing to get a couple fingers on my phone while it's still vibrating. The screen reads:

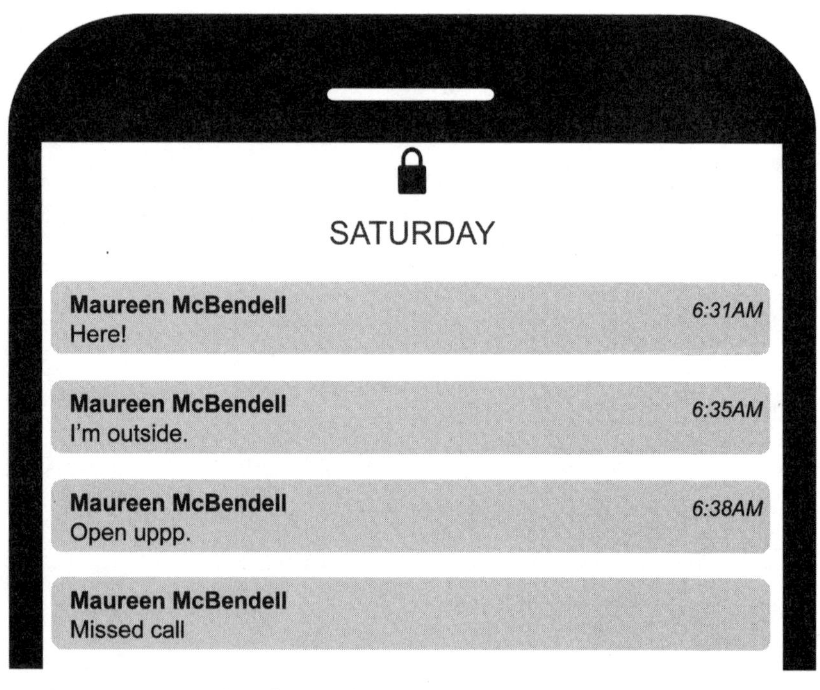

I saunter to the front door then flip up a slat of blinds hanging by the window. Through the crack, I find Mo's blinding glow rushing in, a radiance that truly embodies her aura. She twists the knob on her side of the door the moment I unlock it, welcoming a chilling draft.

"Morning!" she says, greeting me with soft kisses on my chin that lead to my lips, gently brushing the back of her cold hand against the ripe stubble along my cheek. "You okay?"

"Hey," I reply with the slightest smile. "I'm ... I'm fine. Just tired." *Just tired* — that lazy response for how I'm feeling; the two safe words that steer me miles away from her compassion when I'm down.

"Right," says Mo.

"You're here early."

"I–I guess so." She winces. "Figured you needed some cheering up."

"Nah..." I reply, caught in a *serious* yawn, one that has my face and limbs all seized up as I breathe in. "Just some sleep."

She rolls her eyes. "So, you hungry?"

"Mhm."

Mo slips off her moccasins and sweeps past me, strolling along the hallway to the kitchen. I catch a whiff of her raspberry-pomegranate fragrance, fused with the savoury smell of whatever's in the Tupperware she's carrying. She's dressed in grey, floral-printed Capris and a graphic tee that says *Love Is Undefeated* elegantly by the shoulder, beneath a denim jacket that is short by the waist but baggy in the arms. I bet she'd been shivering out there on the porch. Mo's the type to choose fashion over warmth in these winters, every time. "I brought you breakfast," she says, suspecting I'll follow her to the kitchen. "Waffles. I mushed some bananas into the batter."

"Oh."

"Some chocolate chips too!" She snags the maple syrup from the door of my fridge and flips its lid open, then she squeezes it a bunch until it streams onto my plate. "Tell me when," she says merrily with that cheek-dimpling smile that makes the heavens sing.

I catch myself for a moment, musing at how beauty's so effortless for her. Light curls stream along both sides of her jawline and bounce off her cheeks whenever she turns her head. The way she could show up at my doorstep without a smudge of makeup on and her hair wrapped into that messy-yet-still-perfect bun will always catch my eye.

"When," I say, delicately, knifing into the mountain of crispy, golden, grid-pressed cakes.

Mo snaps the lid closed and wipes a sticky blob of syrup running off my plate. She smears it across her lips. "So..."

"So."

"So how was training this week?"

"Early."

"Like, 'early in the morning' early, or 'next season's starting earlier than expected' early?"

"Is a basketball round, or does it bounce?"

She purses her lips for a reply, then hesitates, hearing my apathy for this conversation. "*Oh.* I see," she says, wrapping herself around my arm, tilting her cheek onto my shoulder — that endearing, consoling thing she does that insinuates *everything will be all right* if I'm by her side. As though warm cuddles could be the gold standard fix for sour moods.

What she cannot realize is that I am not tired, or sore, or wanting to be consoled, or even griping about the unprecedented training regimen that Arlen's got us into.

"All the more reason why next season'll be your best," she assures me. "Y'know, heaps of time to improve!"

Uh-huh. I'm astounded at how she's so oblivious to my dying appetite, the despondence in my eyes, the fidgeting urge that's burning me inside. I've yet to spill what's been weighing me down for so long. Around and around goes my fork, handled loosely. It swirls up and down and paints loopy patterns in the runny syrup.

"They taste all right?" asks Mo. "Too grainy?" *No, they're scrumptious, Mo. Delectable, really.* "I had to use whole-grain flour 'cause I ran out of waffle mix," she says. "Oh! And I mixed in a pinch of cinnamon, since—"

"I don't think I wanna play anymore."

"Wait, what?"

"I'm ... I'm serious, Mo."

She stops herself in her tracks, wondering how to settle the depressive air lingering so thickly around me.

"You're just feeling down from that game the other day. It was Wednesday, right?" Mo asks. "Give it some—"

"I don't need *time* to make sense of how I feel."

"But next season'll be your—"

"Heard you the first time, Mo."

"You don't wanna do this."

"I do."

"You sure? Basketball's your life."

"I am. And it *was*."

"I understand, love."

"You don't."

"Oh," she responds, at a loss for words to make things right, struggling to accept that she can't empathize with my ordeal. Not this time, at least. "Well," she says, shrugging, "if I can't understand what's up with you, then who could?"

I shrug back.

She asks, "Your fam—"

"Not a chance."

"A teammate?"

I sigh, shaking my head.

"Umm..." Mo ponders. "What about a..."

"A *what*?"

She's stammering, wincing when I raise an eyebrow. "A professional? Someone you could talk to. Like, I dunno, a therapist or something."

I'm thrown aback. *A shrink*! *Are you kidding me, Mo*?

"So what, I'm crazy now?"

"Who says you gotta be crazy to see a therapist? You haven't been yourself lately, even before you lost earlier this week. You've been..."

"I've been ... I've been *what,* Mo?"

"Off."

"Off?"

"Yes, *off.* You've been off. Now's starting to feel a lot like déjà vu from a couple years ago, y'know, when you—"

"You don't gotta remind me!"

"Okay, okay." Mo gazes solemnly into my eyes. She slides her hands over mine to interlock our fingers. "Talk to someone. For me. Please."

I look away and to the window, trying to somehow escape this intervention. I could just picture Mo telling me, "It's okay to not be okay," wanting me to "talk about my feelings" and whatnot — which, don't get me wrong, is all fine for people willing to get into all of that, but just not me. I wasn't raised talking about when or why I felt empty, or lost and confused, or afraid of letting go of a part of me that made me, *me.* I never had those talks. Not with family. So, definitely not with teammates or anyone else. It wasn't my thing.

Mo cups her soft palm against my cheek, gently pulling me in. As our eyes meet, I find worry all over her face. "Please," she goes. "For me."

DAYS LATER

It's strange how you can grow so heavily acquainted with an aspect of your life that you've held so dearly to your heart. An aspect that you thought you knew so thoroughly and innately, so much so that you wouldn't be yourself without it. You spend your entire life devoted to this one thing, and along the journey, the hardships and pains and struggles have a subtle way of distancing you from *you* — the *you* that you thought you were. Then one day, you're slapped in the face by something that obliterates your reality as you know it, until you realize you've entirely lost the concept of who you are or that aspect of your life you thought you knew so well.

I find similarities when roaming around the McInnis Centre.

I'd swipe my student ID for access past the barriered front entrance; take the stairs up a few flights past the university's illustrious shrine, where the tall banners and gleaming trophies reside; hang a right to enter the long hallway of team locker rooms, with its glossy green walls painted over concrete brick, and then *voilà*: at the end of the hallway, the shiny glass doors on the left should read, *McINNIS CENTRE OF ATHLETICS AND RECREATION — MAIN COURT*. There you have it: the same route to the gym, mapped out with directions that, for a while now, have been engrained in my head. The same route that imbues McInnis with a true sense of the term, *second home.*

I thought I knew McInnis inside and out.

Until today.

Until I felt embarrassed asking the receptionist at the front desk, "Which way to Doctor Feldbrook's office?"

Until she replied, "Past the front entrance, up the stairs to the third floor, past the labs and to the right of the coaches' lunchroom. Should be one of those doors," and I figured that I had hardly known the facility at all.

* * *

I pace through the hallway—wary of a possible Maythorn sighting — and find the teal-coated door that reads, *ARCHIBALD FELDBROOK, Ph.D. Psychology, Faculty of Sport Science*, and under that, *Varsity Athlete Advisor*, in shiny lettering. *What am I getting myself into*? I wonder, idling by his door.

Here goes nothing. Thump-thump-thump...

"Come in," he says.

I enter an office painted a soft powder green. It's spatially neat in here: the furniture is placed like islands resting above a sea of pepper-tiled flooring; but the loose files across his desk and atop his bookshelf juxtapose with the orderliness.

"Mister Clendon. Tough loss last week. To what do I owe this pleasure?"

Coldly, I ask, "This psychiatry thing free?"

"I wouldn't know. Seeing as I'm not a psychiatrist," he goes. "But yes, it's free. Advisory sessions won't cost you a dime."

"Cool."

"I've been expecting you for quite some time, Mister Clendon, believe it or not. Do you know why you're here?"

"Well, I..." Where do I begin? "No."

He removes his glasses and looks at me, shuffling a handful of marked-up exams against his desk and storing them away. Then he says, "You have all the tools, kid. You're smart. You're gifted athletically. I've been following basketball here for quite some time now, though I've never seen an athlete of your ability step foot on campus."

"Loving this shower of compliments, man."

"Well," he says, pulling out the guest seat, "allow me to turn the faucet shut. You didn't perform up to par this season."

"I know."

"Something's going on in your head, but what is it? First-year growing pains or whatnot? Why are you here?"

I mutter, "You tell me."

"Hmm?"

"You're the shrink. Can't you figure that out?"

He sighs, reading the indifference on my face, hearing

the disdain in my tone. He doesn't gotta be a psych expert to realize I'm not thrilled about any of this.

"Okay. Well, my door's always open, Udoka. For both your entry and exit. You don't need to be here."

"Great," I groan, gathering my backpack and folding my bomber jacket over my forearm. "My bad for knocking."

"If you do what you've always done, then you'll get what you've always gotten."

"What?"

"Sport is profoundly a mental game. What separates the mediocre from the good, even the good from the exceptional, lies nowhere but between the ears. Now, I know why you're here. I'm just waiting for you to say it."

"I don't know why, man."

"All right," he says with a chuckle. "Good luck next season."

"Is this shit funny to you?"

"Is what shit?"

"This!" I exclaim.

He smirks. "Do clarify."

"Am I a joke to you?"

"Not in the least. But that ego you brought into my office a moment ago, storming in here like you're above and beyond a visit," he says, chuckling once more, "seeing it now, as bruised as it is, frankly it's quite hilarious. I'll ask again..." He clears his throat. "Why are you here?"

My head hangs as I stare into the patterns on the floor, trying to let go of my guarded, hollowing self-esteem that he's made the topic of laughter. I respond under my breath, "Confidence."

"Speak up."

"Confidence," I repeat.

"What about it?"

"My confidence! I'm here 'cause I lost it, man. It's messin' with my game."

"Yes!" he shouts. "Yes! The first step is acknowledging the problem, embracing the problem, coming face-to-face with the problem and telling it, 'You may have me beat right now, but I will conquer you!'" He rises from his seat, reaching over and offering his hand. "Archie Feldbrook," he says. "It'd be my pleasure to help you, kid."

It may as well be time to confide in someone other than Mo. Maybe she's right. Whether whatever I'm getting myself into can help me see things clearer, I oughta feel brave for trying. For sharing, in the least, just a glimpse of what I've been through and how it has affected me and my love for the game. Was Wednesday's game my last? I don't know.

But it may be time to open up.

Transparently. Vulnerably. Finally.

CHAPTER IV

THE THOUGHT THAT COUNTS

Glimmering on Feldbrook's index finger is a gold ring that I believe says *CHAMPIONS OF 1980*-something, with an embroidered baseball on the front and tiny stones all around it. He's dressed in a corduroy blazer over a beige, collared shirt with the buttons loosened at the neck. Shallow wrinkles run across his pale forehead, his scalp and tidy beard sprinkled grey. Resting on his nose is a bulky pair of frameless, thick-lensed reading glasses. He seems unbothered, unhurried, unconcerned about the eternity he's been taking — reclining in his chair and sipping from his Wolfpack mug. I mean, it's not like we only have a half-hour session, but sure, Doc, sip away.

Meanwhile, there's me, feeling restless and edgy and

unsure of how to get this thing going, whatever this is. We'll be sitting here mute this whole time if he doesn't say something first, because I surely won't.

"Tell me something about yourself," he goes, *finally*. "I mean, something you've hidden from the people closest to you."

I rest my backpack on the bland tile floor, leaning it against the chair. I'm puzzled thinking about how to put a finger on my entwined thread of problems. "Like what?"

"Maybe family, I suppose?" He squints. "Yeah, let's begin there."

"What about it?"

"Anything. Parents, siblings, anyone." He shrugs and scrunches his face as though to say, *Gimme something to build on, something to reach with.* An incident, a family feud, a petty argument that lingered into something more damaging than it was ever intended to be. He's waiting for me to blurt out something that he can grab hold of and untangle, and I guess whatever happened back home where I grew up is where he'll start picking at the knot. "How were they back then, when you were little?"

"They were cool."

"'Were whom, might I ask?"

"Umm ... my—"

"Let's begin with Dad. How was he during those times?" I can feel my face quivering. Feldbrook's voice hoarsened with regret the moment "dad" seeped from his mouth.

"He..." I sigh, deeply. "Well, Pop. He was a good—"

Before I can take another breath, Feldbrook clicks open his pen, asking, "Better yet, how about Mom?"

"Ma, she was..." a profound benchmark of nurture, someone who would continually raise the bar for what is meant by maternal love. She taught me empathy and compassion and the value of saying what you mean and meaning what you say. She was everything and more to me back then, and she still is to this day. The greatest, most caring mom in the world. But I'd be lying if I were to say she's not at least partially the reason I'm sitting here, all tense and embarrassed, in front of this psychologist or psycho-whatever, who insists I vent about my confidence issues on the court. "She was *nice*."

"Nice," he replies, "that's *nice*, descriptive. Was she — I dunno — supportive?"

"Toward what, basketball stuff?"

"Yeah, your basketball stuff," he says. "Was she?"

"Well..." Reaching for any memories involving Ma and "my basketball stuff," immediately I realize there's only a scarce collection of them coming to mind. I mean, she was far more than supportive. Like I said: Ma nurtured me, through and through. She often seemed flustered with concern for who or what I'd become, fretting over whether I'd grow into everything she'd wished for in a son.

When I was little, she made sure my knapsack was supplied with blank notebooks and sharpened pencils, so that I was well-equipped for the first days of grade school every year. Amid those chilly September mornings, Ma would crouch toward me, her voice ringing with the brisk breeze. "Be good today, my love. Make Mummy proud. Remember the three Ps of success: *preparation, preparation, preparation*!" she'd exclaim, warmly but sternly, as I'd drift away from her sentiments and toward the dinging school bell.

I supposed she'd ruminate about what I'd learn throughout the day, or whether I was well-behaved, or whether her mantra had resonated with me and steered me toward sound decisions — because surely, she'd inquire about all of the above by dinnertime. But there at the dinner table, she'd dismiss my babbling about the baskets I scored during recess, or the friendships I forged with the other Black kids in my class because of the orange, pebbly ball she cared so little about. Trivial, sure. Yet her disinterest lingered throughout my adolescence when she'd drop me off for a tournament but hardly stay to watch me play. Ma had other priorities, of course: a home to manage, chores to enforce, meals to prepare, a career to maintain — commitments I would understand as I aged.

So in the following years, when I'd come home from a game, having Ma greet me without a concern for how

I played but mention that she had saved me a hearty serving of leftovers, since she knew I'd be starving — I'd give her the benefit of the doubt.

But not *always*.

Because often she'd relay what she saw on the news as she wound down late at night: the recap of crimes and misdeeds, the latest in politics, the unpredictable economy, and if not already dozed off, the brief sports segment that was notably unamusing to her but became a topic of discussion only whenever I was around and the NBA or college hoops were being mentioned. "Look, Udoka! Isn't that what's-his-name? You played with him, right? Or against him, was it? Look at him on TV, jumpin' around and all that! When're you gonna be on TV?" she'd obliviously tease. "When're you gonna get an M-C-double-A scholarship to the States, too? They're handing out full rides like candy now!"

"It's *N*-C-double-A, Ma," I'd tell her. "And I dunno, maybe ask a scout or two. Lemme know what they say 'bout me."

"No, for real! There's a heap of kids playing down south now! C'mon, Udoka, don't let my efforts go to waste. It took a lot to raise you! When's it all gonna pay off?"

I'd grind my teeth and scowl from behind her, dismissing the banter with something like, "Dinner?"

"What?"

"Were you able to fix me a plate, Ma?"

"Yes, darling. Shepherd's pie and sautéed greens. Left it in the oven to keep warm. Why didn't you look first? You know where I leave it for you."

"Thanks," I'd mutter, imagining how different things could've been. If only she'd been attentive to *me* at the dinner table when I was younger, sharing a glimpse of my wish to one day glimmer on her TV in some flashy jersey — she probably would've known that I related only to the schoolmates who looked like me and shared the same hopes too; and she would've grasped that not *everyone's* childhood pipe dream could come to fruition so easily. If only she'd wished me "good luck" from the first row of the bleachers, instead of from the driver's seat of her sedan before running errands — she'd get to witness a few games and come to realize how competitive Canadian basketball was becoming, at a time when there was still very little scouting from Division 1 coaches here, compared to their own home-grown talent. If only she'd known how thoughtless or annoying it was of her to ask when I'd get my opportunity when she didn't experience me chasing my dream herself — she'd probably bite her tongue instead, because she would've known how badly I wanted to have her "efforts pay off," even when they weren't.

But it was okay.

Because after I'd stumble into the house after a hard-fought game, there it was — a nourishing, full-course meal just waiting for me, so I could refuel for the next day of hoops. Ma did support me, no question. I can't begin to fathom what or where I'd be without her.

* * *

"Well," says Feldbrook. "Was she?"

"Hmm?"

"Was your mom supportive of your basketball?"

"Yeah, she was. Still is, too. In her *own* way."

"What else was she back then?"

"Anxious. Paranoid about virtually anything."

Feldbrook raises an eyebrow. "Oh."

"Watching the evening news was her thing. She'd absorb all the details of who had been stabbed or robbed, or what foods made so-and-so sick, or why you shouldn't buy such-and-such because this young married couple from whichever town got scammed because of this or because of that," I tell him. "I can picture Ma in front of her TV, stooped at the edge of her seat, sipping her steaming Earl Grey before hollering something bizarre from across the house like, 'Did you hear about the family that got carbon monoxide poisoning? The remote key turned their car on in their garage!' to which I'd lie and holler back, 'Yeah, Ma! Crazy, I know.'"

Feldbrook nods steadily, a purring emanating from his mouth while he sips from his mug. "And the meaning of it all — how do you find yourself impacted?"

"She insisted I be careful, vigilant, wary of all things in life that have threatened the livelihood or wellbeing of *someone, anyone* in the history of society, anywhere, in any way. For that, she led a certain lifestyle. A safe life. A danger-free life that she felt was her duty to project onto me and my sister. She often shied away from taking risks, from exposing herself to unfamiliar experiences that could've changed her life for better or worse. She preferred a mundane, obedient way of living. My mum would encourage me to 'shoot for the stars' or 'aim for the big bucks' — two of the clichés she'd use. But…"

"But?"

"But ironically, she favoured a more sheltered, conventional life. Ma endorsed the perks of a plan B, as if any ordinary lifestyle was worth dreaming about."

"As for basketball, why are you *here*?"

"She indoctrinated me into her world of … fear."

"Fear. Hmm…" Feldbrook ponders, his gaze drifting to the ceiling as though the patterns on the drywall could map out the complexities of my brain. "Of what?"

"Unfortunate events. Dangerous things. Y'know, *bad stuff*."

"Oh."

"Since I was young, her influence drew me away from the risks in the world — until a life exposed to those unfortunate events, those dangerous things, became inevitable."

"So, what does that mean?"

"Means that early on, I lived a life censored from anything that could've challenged my strength, that could've defined my character. She shielded me from life's unavoidable obstacles. So much so that when I had to face adversity, I had no clue how to handle it or what it'd do to me."

He waits a moment before he replies, "So?"

"So, I avoided it. Until I couldn't anymore."

"So?"

"So, *what*!" I exclaim.

"So, what! Exactly! So, what does that mean to you? What's that have to do with basketball?"

"*So*, when Maythorn demands we stick to the game plan, I listen. I keep my game simple. Straightforward. Risk-free."

"All right..."

"Whereas my teammates — they abide, sure, but with the courage, or confidence or whatever, to bend Maythorn's orders just enough to suit their own game. How it *should* be for me, too. When I'm out there, I feel obliged to make the easy pass instead of threading the needle to a cutting teammate for a score, since I know there's a chance the pass could get stolen. Obliged to play honest, patient defense, instead of gambling for a steal that could be misread, and having fingers being pointed at me for giving up an open shot. Obliged to stick to the play-call, even when I see a lane that may have some traffic but is nothing that a crossover or spin move couldn't counter. When I'm out there, Doc, I feel obliged to conform. *Afraid* to play my game."

"Well, what happens when your pass gets intercepted, or ... or you miss a steal and get scored on, or lose control of the ball?"

"I feel the mistake. The team feels it, too. Maythorn has a fit, and then—"

"So..." *If this snappy old man says "so" one more time!* "Then what? Do you get cut from the team? Do you collapse and die? Does the world end?"

"No!" I shout. "I'm not tryna make this bigger than it is! But it's the fear that I feel, the voice in my head telling me, 'Don't do it! Don't you dare!' or, 'You shouldn't've tried that move! Now look what happened!' That stupid voice ... it pesters me whenever I think about playing *my game*."

"Your game, you say."

"Yeah. *My game.* I lost sight of what it was. It won't come back. I guess that's why. *That's why* I'm here."

CHAPTER V

HOMECOURT

Feldbrook fiddles with his mug, twirling its round base against his paper-strewn desk. He stares into the empty, coffee-stained cylinder as though he'd like to get up for a refill, but he seems hesitant to budge. And I hope he doesn't, because whatever he's doing to extract these pent-up frustrations from my head is surely a relief. These frustrations, these deep, dark feelings, the ones to which I never thought of consciously giving meanings — they're all in the air now. It's like he's somehow prying open this door to the maze of my psyche — a door that had been closed long before I knew there was something on the other side. This whole "therapy" thing was foreign and certainly pointless to me just days ago, but hey, here I am. Who knows, maybe this won't be too bad after all.

"What about Pop?" asks Feldbrook.

"Like I said, Doc. He was good to me."

"Then why'd you seem so troubled when he was brought up? How was your relationship with him, your childhood with him?"

"Well, back then, Pop was ... demanding. See, Pop believed in me more than I had ever believed in myself. He felt that I could do anything. *Anything*! So, it must've frustrated him whenever I gave the impression that I didn't feel the same way. I couldn't always agree with his plans for me either, especially 'cause *he* dictated how I should've chased my dreams, without a care for how I felt about reaching them myself."

"But?"

"But looking back, how could I ever resent him for wanting nothing but the best for me?"

"I get it. What sort of things would happen, though?"

"Well, from time to time, I catch myself reliving moments from our road trips. We'd be on our way home from a game or tourney or whatnot. I was nine, ten, maybe eleven years old in the back seat. Bashing the steering wheel, with a heavy foot on the gas, in this irritated tone he'd ask something like, 'Why couldn't you score more?' or 'What's up with all the times you threw the damn ball away?' or whatever."

"How did that make you feel?"

"Not like smiling, I can tell you that much."

"Oh," says Feldbrook.

"I wouldn't hear the end of it if I had a bad outing, even if my team won. And if I played a solid game, he'd rarely share his congrats."

"What did that do to you?"

"I guess it all developed into some sort of ... complex," I confess, letting out a shallow breath. "As I got older, I began to understand his reasons, though. His expectations for me were always through the roof. But back when I was younger, the things he'd do to get the best out of me — they did more harm than good. They led me to believe I was never good enough. I thirsted for a *'Great game, man,'* or a *'Better luck next time, I'm still proud of you,'* every now and then, but a drop of praise barely left the spout."

"Must've been tough to accept, especially at such a young age," says Feldbrook. He quickly looks over his shoulder at the analog clock behind him, where both hands point straight to the ceiling. Startled by the time, he flips his wristwatch to confirm it. "When're we scheduled 'til?"

"Twelve fifteen."

"Yes. Yes, yes. Right," he says. "Got class?"

"Yeah. Well, sort of. Tutorial at twelve thirty. This elective I'm taking."

"Got it. Now, please," says Feldbrook, his hands weaving under his arms, "do continue with the family dynamic. Any siblings?"

"Yeah, there's my sister, Leena. And—"

"Younger, older?"

"Younger. Four years younger than me."

"Lovely. You two get along? What about her and Pop?"

"Nah, they..." My mouth starts quivering. The thought of Leena and Pop being mentioned in the same breath gets me tense. "They hardly saw eye to eye, man. They were always caught up in some feud. I ... I, um..."

"You *what*?"

"I felt guilty from time to time."

"And why's that?"

"Pop devoted tons of time to my basketball thing. *No*, he wasn't always cool about it, and *yes*, we sparred over a bunch of problems, but there wasn't a doubt in my mind that he cared. With Leena, things were different. He showed interest in whatever she was into, but it always seemed more dutiful than genuine. Never real or organic. I think I was to blame for that."

"Surely, it wasn't your fault, kid," Feldbrook casually assumes, dismissing what I felt was the rock that struck glass and shattered a perfect family portrait of smiles and matching knitted sweaters. The rock that ruined the picture forever and left shards scattered on the floor. The rock that I must've thrown. The *rock* that I've dribbled and shot for years, actually. *Don't tell me it's not my fault.*

"The countless hours that Pop and I had shared — they

stirred Leena's resentment toward him. Seeing his face in the stands at all my practices and workouts and games meant he was absent for Leena's recitals and plays. At the dinner table, Pop would marvel about a move I pulled on some kid, but he never gave kudos to Leena for landing a role in the school musical or nailing the moves for a new dance routine. She'd be downcast, picking at her food, quietly awaiting a shout-out for what she'd done. Yet Pop would only yap about a petty crossover that I had worked on all week to get more baskets. I felt helpless."

Feldbrook, now peeling back the many layers of the reason for *why I'm here*, solemnly asks, "Where was your mom through it all?"

"Ma worked at the hospital. Y'know, the one by Kensington Market?"

"Toronto Western," he confirms.

"Yeah, that one. She tried getting involved in my extracurriculars. I mean, whenever she could, but whatever. Leena's, too. But as for Pop, it was like Leena didn't fit into his box of interests. She felt forgotten. I was too absorbed in my own ambitions to consider the impact it had on her."

"What else didn't you consider?"

"How ungrateful I was." Feldbrook gives me a puzzled look. "Everything Pop put into my hoops thing would be in vain if I quit now."

Shaking his head sympathetically, Feldbrook goes, "You can't blame yourself, Udoka."

"Who's to say Leena wouldn't be dancing, or singing, or even acting out in some movie right now if Pop supported her as much as he supported me?"

"No one. No one at all," he asserts. "And that's no knock on your sister, either. Woulda, coulda, shouldas are as infinite as they are negligible." Feldbrook sways back and forth in his chair. "Time?"

I lean to the side for a better look at the clock. "Couple minutes past twelve."

"Cool. Keep an eye on it! Teaching a lecture across campus at twelve thirty, too."

"Gotcha."

"Any other memory that stood out?"

"Yeah, this one trip home. Can't forget it."

"More critiquing from Pop?"

"No," I tell him, "not this time. I was probably fifteen, riding shotgun. Had a Gatorade sealed to my lips like a pacifier to a baby. Must've had, I dunno, maybe thirty-five points in the game I just played, tired and all. Pop was super thrilled about my huge game, so we stopped at an out-of-town diner before returning home that evening. He treated me to ice cream as this huge congrats."

"That must've meant a lot."

"Oh, *the universe,*" I reply assuredly. "I brought out a youthful side of him that day, a joy he often concealed. It was ... it was everything."

"*Everything* … meaning?"

"Well, it meant way more than droppin' a thirty-ball! Making him proud was all I cared about, really."

"Right, right. Yes." Feldbrook leans over facing me, his eyes racing left and right and reading the subtle wretchedness in my brows, my cheeks, the clenches in my jaw. "So, what happened?" he asks, resting his pen on his desk, inviting me to continue…

PAST

We sat in cherry-red seats. Pop was all smiles, telling me what ran through his mind when I tried *this* move or how loud he cheered when I made *that* shot. He must have kept his eyes peeled to the action whenever I checked in, like he always did, and I'd known this by the elaborate play-by-play he shared at the table. Catching glares from nearby guests when babbling something like, "That turnaround jumper was sweet!" or mimicking the shimmies I had used, while hollering, "You killed 'em with your 'tween-the-legs hesi! Had 'em on skates all day long," I couldn't help but smile through the embarrassment. I was witnessing a warm reminder that despite his tough love and often absent encouragement, Pop was still my number one fan. And I appreciated him for that, for how deeply invested he was in watching every play of every game. I saw him glimmer with joy, a blinding gleam of pride that could've brightened that entire spot.

Pop placed an order for a hot fudge brownie sundae with nothing less than thirty-five chocolate chips sprinkled over it, and I remember this specifically because of the curious, *what-the-hell* look that the waiter gave him. But Pop shrugged it off. "Dinner is dinner," he said.

Throughout the diner were pockets of empty beer bottles hanging upside-down from the ceiling. Hung against the glossy black walls were simple paintings housed in simple frames. There were also several wide flat-screen TVs; each was equally as massive as its neighbour but hung at such a height from the tables that you'd need to squint from virtually anywhere to catch a good view.

We caught the first half and a bit of the third quarter of a playoff game, although the score at the bottom-right corner of each TV was nearly impossible to see. It was only before a timeout or commercial break when the scoreboard would hit centre-screen during a slow-motion clip of the highlights.

"Finally!" I said. "There it is. Fifty-one, forty-three for the Purple and Gold."

Pop replied, "How much time on the clock?"

"About seven thirty left in the third."

"*Seven thirty*?" he gasped.

"I guess neither team could buy a bucket." Pop patted down his vest, the zippered pouch in his sweater, the side and back pockets in his jeans. "What's up with you?" I asked, baffled.

"Time?"

"Seven ... seven thirty."

"No!" he shrieked. "*The time*!"

I gathered my phone, beginning to worry when I realized it couldn't catch the local reception for some reason. "Five past eight," I said. "What's going on?"

"I got the bill," he replied, all panicky. "We gotta go. Now. Like, *right now*!"

We hit the road and sped onto the 400 heading south to get wherever we were going, mulling over vastly different motives: me — chomping at the bit to tell Ma and Leena all about my huge game; and Pop — I thought, then and there — troubled by something he couldn't afford to forget.

* * *

I was lurched awake by the speed bump we rode over. We pulled up at the front entrance of this mighty building. Waiting behind a tall pair of sliding doors was Ma.

I wanted to say, "Eh, Ma! Look what I got!" with a steady rise in pitch. I planned to reach beneath my hoodie for the medal that I'd won, running my thumbs against the embroidered words, *TOURNAMENT ALL-STAR*, swishing the shiny ribbon proudly around my neck.

But that didn't happen.

And instantly, the exuberance was wiped off my face.

I saw that whole scenario disappear into thin air and felt silly — embarrassed, even — for picturing a happy, candid, basketball-related moment with Ma, without another clash between her and Pop. I felt robbed of the idyll.

Because immediately, I noticed she'd been crying.

She was in her polka-dot scrubs and we, Pop and I, hadn't just arrived at any mighty building — we'd arrived at her place of work, the hospital, nearly two hours after the end of her twelve-hour shift.

I slid my passenger window down and slowly found her scowling from outside the car. "Where were you guys?" she cried, her cheeks daubed with dried tears.

Oh, I thought. *Seven thirty*. I hadn't known. I wanted to reply, "*Out of town, Ma. I had a tourney today.*" I wanted to provide some explanation, even while suppressing everything I'd been dying to share about my game and how well I'd played.

But I couldn't.

Because it wasn't my place to do that — and although I wanted to take on some of the blame, it wasn't my responsibility either.

"It's friggin' nine twenty-three! Where were you guys!" Ma screeched. She poked her head through the passenger window and surveyed the rear seats. "And where's Leena! Why the hell isn't she with you two!"

"She's at that vocal recital," Pop responded, "you forget?"

"What the hell do you mean, 'You forget?' I reminded *you* about it before you two dropped me off this morning and took the car to go God-knows-where! It's always *basketball this, basketball that*. Leena matters too, did *you* forget?"

Pop shrugged. "Of course not."

"What about how Leena's recital was *last* weekend? Yeah — the one she missed because you were late getting home from Udoka's game? Or what about her sleepover last night at Ella's for *her* out-of-town audition earlier today, huh? What about that!"

"At Ella's?"

"Yes! *Ella*, her friend from school! Sound familiar? What about how she should've been practicing her lines with Ella from this morning? But she couldn't since her script was buried in the front seat! It had these ... all these basketball diagrams scribbled over it!" Ma ripped open the passenger door and clawed through the glove compartment to find the script in the exact state she'd described. "Here it is!" She crumpled it into a ball, scrunching it tighter and tighter before flinging it at Pop's face. "Did *you* forget!" she screamed.

"Ma!" I yelled, resisting her tussling into the car.

"Ella's parents let Leena stay with them 'til after

the audition but were gonna drop her home — *home* — afterwards, since they had somewhere to be!" She pounded the nearest headrest, battling for composure. "Any of this ring a bell? Or did the thought of Leena's whereabouts not cross your mind at all, let alone getting *here* on time?"

Pop was speechless. Seemingly unapologetic, but speechless.

"No. It didn't," Ma continued. "Because all that did was that basketball play-thing you were going on about before dropping me off this morning. The *give-and-dash*, or whatever it's called, and how it could get Udoka more baskets."

I peered over at Pop, studying the indifference in his demeanour, anticipating how he'd sculpt his apology or excuse. "It's *give-n-go*," he muttered, "the *play-thing*. Give. And. Go."

Ma jerked open the backseat door. She stormed into the sedan and slammed the door shut.

"He had thirty-five!" he pleaded.

When questioned about what took so long, Pop connived his way out of the fault. "Why you gotta be so selfish?" he brashly asked whenever Ma complained — as though he and I were entitled to the Corolla for out-of-town trips on Ma's workdays; as though arriving on time for Ma after her day of treating sick people was too burdensome a task; as though Ma was wrong and audacious even to question Pop's responsibilities that night.

At times I would peek over at Ma through the rear-view mirror, fixating on the despair in her eyes that streamed down her rosy cheeks. I felt helpless but complicit in Pop's negligence. But away from Ma's reflection, and toward the cars and streetlights and dimly lit buildings that passed, was where I set my eyes — as though everything was fine and ordinary.

Just like the other times.

Because this time wasn't the first.

And although it wasn't Pop's disinterest in her affairs but rather Ma's anguish for him that churned my stomach — I was, at that point, completely accustomed to Ma's grief.

So, there I was — caught in the crossfire of yet another family struggle. Whether Pop versus Leena or Pop versus Ma, it all spawned the same ache in my heart. My passion for basketball — a mutual pastime between Pop and I that brought me closer to him, to *Her* — all came at the expense of tearing the family apart. I thought it was an unfair dilemma, since I was too young to have taken a side, let alone fathom there'd been a fence that divided us.

PRESENT

"*Her*?" asks Feldbrook.

I nod. "Yes."

He stares at me blankly.

I can remember when it all started. The day my life began revolving around an air-filled leather sphere. It was at Woolner Park where Ma sat with me, the lone picnic table by the ball courts near the dog park. The table was glutted with all the finger foods imaginable and a few cupcakes each with four narrow candles poking out of them. My feet dangled above the grass. The delight of hearing those baby carrots snap between my front teeth was everything and more.

I heard, "Got something for you!" and knew it was Pop calling from a distance. I turned to the hollow sound of a ball bouncing against the pavement then swishing through the grass as it rolled to my feet. Pop raced over, hoping to catch my reaction. I asked, "What's this?" and he said, "My gift to you. Happy birthday!"

He plucked the ball from the grass and twirled it on the axis of his finger, which seemed quite literally like magic before my eyes. "Whoa..." I mused; my fascination was transfixed by Her allure. Pop tapped the ball over and over to keep it spinning, concentrating keenly on its momentum. He said, "She could be your destiny. She could take you places — around the globe, even. If you work hard, if you treat Her right. But if you don't," he tapped the ball less and less frequently, then not at all, letting it wobble and fall to the ground — "everything could stop spinning for you. But don't worry, I'll be there. Wherever you and Her wander. *I promise*."

Pop knelt and placed the ball in the bowl of my tiny palms. I tried spinning it just as he did, only to have my finger collapse against its weight. I tried again, and another time, and of course found no luck but imagined myself one day having it spin as perfectly as he made it, one day taking myself around the world with "Her," just like he'd said. That ball wasn't what I'd expected as a birthday gift during then — which might've been a G.I. Joe set or some LEGO bricks or what have you — but I didn't mind. Not even in the slightest. For Pop's gift, I thought, inspecting its rough, pebbly surface — *She* was perfect.

* * *

I look at Feldbrook as sternly as the first time he'd questioned me. "Yes," I reassert. "*Her*. The game. Basketball."

"Okay," Feldbrook mutters, looking puzzled. "Yes, sure. *Her*. Basketball. But like I said, you can't blame yourself for being a kid, for dreaming, for idolizing superstars and wanting to be like them one day."

I shrug.

"Is basketball — sorry, *She* — to blame for disrupting the family dynamic? Are you?" he asks — rhetorically, I assume. "We all aspire to reach whatever our goals or dreams may be. You're not at fault for that. Not at all."

"So why, then..." I flush my hands down my face. "Why am I regretting even the *thought* of hangin' 'em up for good?"

"I mean, despite popular belief, athlete burnout *is* in fact a real thing, y'know," Feldbrook scoffs. "You've been playing since — wait, how old?"

"Four. So that's it. Burnout. Just that."

"My lazy, everything'll-be-fine diagnosis — yeah. Burnout. Just that." He chuckles, then regains sincerity, saying, "But jokes aside, no. There's something deeper."

"Right."

"Right. So, you have two options: Option A," he begins, lifting his arm like he has something in his hand, "is to reach a clear mind to prep for the upcoming season. Option B," he continues, lifting his other arm, his hands rising and falling like two ends of a balance scale, "is to wrap your head around a life without basketball. But if you can't find peace with either choice, things'll just get worse if you ask me."

"Understood," I respond. "Yeah ... okay."

"Well then, good!"

"Good."

Feldbrook asks, "What's the time you have?"

From the back pocket of my fitted jeans, I squeeze out my phone. It displays *12:24 p.m. Ah, damn.* "A bit over a quarter-past," I reply. "Think it's time I head out."

"Yes, yes, of course. Me too."

I slip my fingers through the loop of my backpack and gather it from the ground, rising from my seat before pulling open the door.

"Udoka," he calls, so I halt. "Thank you. For today. And y'know, for all the things you shared with me." I nod, standing mute by his door, frozen in every other part of my body. "It's not easy, kid. Talking about that stuff. So, thank you."

I bow my head and twist the knob. "Yeah. 'Til next time."

CHAPTER VI

THE LOVE AND THRILL

Feldbrook's jotting down notes at a hundred miles an hour. He's heavily fixated on my history with Pop, the intrigue of it all, absorbing every fine detail like the receptive, four-eyed sponge he is.

"So Pop was the bad guy, huh," he comments, to which I don't respond, let alone flinch. Because that wasn't true — perhaps spot-on with Ma's or Leena's truth about him, but not mine. It was oceans away, if you ask me. Feldbrook pries anyway: "Wasn't he?"

"He did all he could to keep me happy. Pop was miles from perfect — but to me, he was everything and more. He devoted hours on end getting to know me, spoiling me with his time."

"So he was a good provider, you're saying?"

"Define that."

"A father who looks after his family. Brings food to the table. Sacrifices himself for the greater good of his spouse and children. That sorta thing — a provider!"

I wince. "I mean, he wasn't..."

"He struggled," Feldbrook cuts in, continuing with his notes. "Didn't he?"

"It's more complicated than—"

"Didn't he."

"I mean, sure. I guess. You could say that. But to me, he was everything a kid would ever want. Who else cared to watch all those late-night games with me, even to give a few pointers during commercials? Who else coached me from the bleachers for every game and practice, despite the glares from the parents and the things they'd say among themselves?"

"Seems like Pop satisfied your wants, rather than your needs."

"Basketball was and still remains a necessity in my life. There's no distinguishing between what I've wanted and needed. How could I separate the two?"

"So, then, what fuels your resentment for him?"

"He ... he left. He left me, man. High and dry," I hear myself whimpering, a crackle in my voice.

"Oh, no ... that must've broken you down quite a bit."

"A bit. Hah!"

"Will forgiveness ever come about?"

Forgiveness, he asks. Hmm. "Well, Pop introduced me to my first love. He gave my life meaning. For that, how could I not forgive him? Better yet, what even is there to forgive?"

"Well, why haven't you two made amends, then?"

"I ... well, I..."

"Breathe," Feldbrook murmurs.

"As I was saying, it's more complicated than that."

"Okay. Yes, yes. Of course. But thinking back to your days playing basketball — your memories, your experiences, etcetera — Pop had an impact, correct?"

"Uh-huh." I nod reluctantly. "Very much so."

"So then, basketball-wise, what did he mean to you?"

"Everything. Everything, Doc."

"Please. Do explain!"

I squint at the clock. "You sure?"

"As sure as I'll be."

"All right. Get comfy. It's a long, long story."

He shrugs. "I'm all for it, kid."

"I guess I'll take a trip back to my early youth..."

PAST

From dawn into the late hours of the night, I'd escape to a world that took me to my greatest joys as a child. Sometimes, Pop was right there with me. Other times, I'd cherish my solitude and become whoever I wanted in between those rickety backboards and fading foul lines. Woolner Park was my home, and every moment spent there, with or without Pop, was spent with Her. She and I were inseparable.

Years passed, but my passion for the game remained. So when Pop vanished without a trace of where or why, eventually, my misery settled. Basketball became my outlet for grief. My therapy for sorrow. And because of Pop, who had brought so much pain to my life yet so much purpose, basketball became my love. I began living by the mantra, "Eat, sleep, hoop," with no distractions in between.

Every morning, I'd put up shot after shot before dragging myself to school. The sound of the ball thumping against the rough tarmac or rattling around the rim before a score became my morning song. And oh, how sweet a tune it was.

After school, 'til around sunset, was when the local hoopsters would gather for pickup; some of them I'd soon befriend.

There was Mikey, the dead-eye shooter of the group.

Bray, Mr. Super-athlete — he would jump so high, you'd think he could grab loose coins off the top ledge of the backboard, until the day came when he actually did.

Simeon, who'd seldom come out to play since he was always tangled in some trouble, but when he did suit up and wasn't distracted, he was a force to be reckoned with.

And Keele, a small but pesky guard; he's got some years on the rest of us.

Together, we shared the thrill of competing every evening, battling to outplay each other and fighting for precious bragging rights, even if the score would reset the next day. I'd impose my will on them, regardless of whether the guy in front of me was someone with whom I shared a close friendship. But surely, soon enough, they'd manage to return the favour. See, there was no mercy in between those sidelines. And we honoured that.

We also shared the common goal of playing alongside one another in high school. We had planned on joining Keele by attending Runnymede C.I., with hopes of winning the Toronto District, then the provincial title, then conquering the world, pretty much. That was the plan.

But when Keele decided to transfer to Oakwood, the basketball powerhouse just a forty-minute TTC ride east on St. Clair from his former stomping grounds, it was the end of our clique's title dream and the birth of our own fierce rivalry, because I had joined Keele as his rookie. That collective goal of winning it all was taken from Mikey, Bray, and Simeon — stolen by the two who'd left the bunch. And in my sophomore year, when Keele and I took on Runnymede at Oakwood, that same fiery competition was everything but extinguished, and the sense of betrayal that Mikey, Bray, and Simeon had rightfully felt was just fuel to the flame.

* * *

A thirty-point lead midway through the fourth quarter was poetic justice for the cut-eye looks they gave me when I jogged down the court, and being the game-high scorer was all I needed to nullify their scornful thoughts.

"Keep punishing 'em," said a calm and collected Keele during a timeout. "Let's put 'em away! Francis!" he called down the bench, hollering at our lights-out, catch-and-shoot marksman who'd been cold from behind the arc all game. "Be ready. Imma get you going!"

On the next possession, Keele dribbled down the court with Simeon hounding his every move. He swooshed the ball behind his back near midcourt, eluding Simeon and approaching a broad avenue to the basket. Bray stepped up to clog the lane, so Keele dished the ball to Francis, who was ready in the corner. Open for a blink, Francis caught the ball to the surprise of Simeon rotating over to guard him. He gave a shot fake, getting Simeon to bite, and drove down the baseline for a high-floating shot at the hoop. Out of nowhere, Bray reached the sky to somehow get his fingertips on the ball. It got deflected to Mikey, where a score on the other end seemed promising.

Mikey advanced the ball ahead to a streaking teammate for an open layup, but I intercepted the pass.

Surveying the vacant court ahead, I chucked the ball to Francis, who'd been late running back on defense. Francis chased down the quick up-court pass that would've gone out of bounds had he been a second too late. I dashed down the court too, shouting at Francis, "Glass! Glass! Glass!" hoping he heard me and was willing to toss an alley-oop. That he did — not off the backboard, though. Francis lobbed the ball perfectly; She was suspended in the air.

And then — takeoff. My elbow neared the rim as I reached for the ball. The gym was silent and motionless. In my sight was Her home, bracing itself for a thunderous arrival. I corralled the ball in the palm of my hand, and with all my might, smashed it through the hoop, snapping the nylon mesh.

"*Ahhhhhhhh*!" I yelled, unaware a defender was airborne with me, yet I realized it was Simeon when I landed. I roared in his face, letting him feel how silly a mistake it was to think he'd have a chance jumping with me.

The crowd rose in pandemonium.

"*Let's goooooooo*!" screamed Francis. Keele and my other teammates gathered, forming what seemed like a mosh pit under Runnymede's basket.

Soon after, the ref called a technical foul — either for a delay-of-game, or for being unsportsmanlike, or for taunting, or whatever. I don't remember, nor at the time did it matter. I wasn't typically one to show emotion after a big play, but this time, I was all for the tech! I could've been tossed out of the game for all I cared, and it wouldn't have meant a thing.

After the free throws, after the cheering and hollering, after the crowd had finally simmered, I stole an inbound pass off a deflection then crushed a tomahawk jam on the very next play. Skipping across the sideline with shimmering pride, with unchallenged bravado, I pumped my arms and roared to the crowd while they reciprocated the energy.

PRESENT

"Was Pop there in the stands, too?" asks Feldbrook. "Cheering you on with the rest of the crowd?"

"Nah, he wasn't. When did you tune out, Doc?" He raises an eyebrow, puzzled. "You still with me?"

"Yes! Yes, right. Vanished without a trace. Pardon me." He clears his throat. "Pop equals no-show to big game. Got it."

I give him a gentle glare, shaking my head.

"So then," Feldbrook says impatiently, "Pop? Relevance?"

"Thought you were 'all for' the long, long story?"

He shakes his wristwatch free and reads the time. "Yes, yes. You're right. I'm listening. Proceed."

PAST

Oakwood was buzzing for the next week or so. I mean, for a student body of only about a half-thousand kids, there's no wonder the word got around so quickly. Whether strolling through the halls, hanging out at the cafe, or even waiting by the bus stop, people I didn't even know were prattling on about my dunks from the Runnymede game.

I downright *basked* in the attention — despite the bashful, easily embarrassed type of guy I was. Because I was *it* that week! I relished the thrill of entering any and every room as the topic of discussion.

Now, what's *it*?

It was the feeling of goosebumps running down your neck the moment you heard your name chanted and cheered from the crowd. *It* was the electricity jolting through your body after you made a huge play, while bright lights shone down on you. *It* was the pride, the popularity, the confidence you carried sporting those three letters — OCI — across your chest for everyone to see. For everyone to admire and revere. For everyone to recognize that you'd earned your stripes to play for one of the top hoops programs in the province — better yet, the country altogether. *It* was the hubris that lingered with you like the scent of an expensive cologne. And during that week, I wore *it* like a swagger that couldn't be contested.

"Yoosie!" I heard from down the hallway. I turned to find it was Keele, weaving his way around students, dragging his feet across the corridor in mid-cut socks and slides. Keele was dressed in a white hoodie beneath a throwback Vince Carter jersey — the one with the jagged pinstripes and the legendary yet not-so-fierce Raptor on the front — with matching sweatpants narrowed down the legs.

I spotted Francis flocking over too. He had on a black-on-black tracksuit with one of his many fitted baseball caps, and his basketball kicks were tied loosely by their strings and hung under the strap of his backpack, giving off a mild stench.

I was in a plain crewneck and grey Roots sweatpants that struggled to hug my waist. The sweatpants were stooping just low enough to show the navy and gold stripes on our team shorts that I wore underneath. That day, I sported a vintage Pittsburgh Penguins snapback with the green under brim — despite having no interest in hockey — just so that the goldish logo would match the shorts.

Anyway, Keele finally approached. "Yo! You gotta check this out!" he shouted, shoving his phone in my face.

I squinted at the screen, oblivious to the commotion. Above a video thumbnail it read *BIGTIME POSTER AND BREAKAWAY FLUSH: 6'1" CANADIAN*

UDOKA CLENDON, and at the top of the webpage, it said *Hoopblog*.

"*Yo*, that's me!"

"Eh, this is dope!" added Francis.

"Hell yeah, it is!" Keele exclaimed. My stomach churned with excitement as I scrolled further to find the grainy footage.

Hoopblog.com was a *huge* deal. It was *the site* for everything basketball — high school hoops, college ball, the pros, everything! I supposed this meant my likeness would reach thousands of viewers, if not tens of thousands; and I hoped a handful of them were D-1 coaches who wanted to catch a glimpse of *me*, the mighty-athletic hoopster from north of the border — from Jane and St. Clair, to be exact.

"Peep the slow-mo!" Keele exclaimed. "This'll get you mad likes on the 'net!" My eyes were glued to the screen. I felt my feet twitch like I was still right there on the hardwood, studying the reactions of each person in the gym: the wild antics from my teammates along the sideline; the cloud of humiliation hovering over Simeon and the astounded faces of his teammates; the alluring girl with the dark, curly hair in the red sweater, who, although perched among Runnymede's tiny cheer section in the stands, couldn't help but applaud me in my glory. She was sitting there, all collected and classy yet still managing to catch my eye amid the madness surrounding her. I wondered if I had impressed her, whoever she was.

I also envisioned Pop right there on the screen, wondering what he might've felt among the crowd. What he might've said or what he might've thought had he been there. He always told me it'd take something special to get my name buzzing, to lift my recruitment off the ground; I wondered if he would've thought it was about to take off.

I didn't know what to expect afterward, but I was anxious for my fate to unfold. Little did I think to be careful what I wished for.

CHAPTER VII

TALK A WHOLE LOTTA GAME

The next day was Thursday.

It was an ordinary day for Oakwood's student body, but not Keele and I. Thursdays were our rest days from practice, so after class we'd always spend them at Woolner Park for some quality runs — practically walking distance from where I grew up. And I was always hyped for that, since it meant all but the same sneaker-scuffing, jump-shooting, slam-dunking (well, at least for me) regime, minus the whistles, reversible pinnies and structured play that we'd otherwise tolerate.

Visiting there every so often couldn't shake me from the childhood nostalgia. The nylon mesh hung below the rim and still sang that sweet, sweet jingle after a swish. I smiled looking at the little boy in his tight sweatshirt dribbling along the sideline, watching the full-court runs so he could get a couple shots off while the action was on the other end — I was him some years ago.

The shoulder-height, chain-link fence stood between me and the ball court — the same ball court that housed countless fantasies from my youth. Keele waited by the entrance too. I wondered if he felt the same.

"Look," said Keele, "over there." Near the far nets by the playground were several locals, chatting and lacing up. Out of the frame was the curly-haired, gently clapping beauty from the Runnymede game. She was wearing a grey sweater, plain black leggings, and a loose ponytail that swooshed with the wind whenever she looked away. "Not there!"

"What, man! What's where?"

"There." Keele pointed under one of the baskets, where the remaining members of Woolner Park's original "Fab Five" shot around with unfamiliar faces. Whispers and mutters circulated swiftly. Our presence was known; what was thought of it remained in question.

Mikey approached from the court. "Yoosie!" he hollered. "Jeez! You didn't have to do us like that, fam!"

I simpered, soon to wipe the smirk off my face the moment I spotted Simeon from the corner of my eye.

"Like *what*?" said Keele. "The thirty-point slap?"

"Or the viral highlight reel?" I teased, a taste of

remorse sitting on my tongue. Mikey dashed to the other side of the fence for a friendly embrace, while Bray soon followed along. Simeon, though — he scoped the exchange, as though he'd rather not be reminded of that past week's posterization; as though he'd rather stare from afar. As though he wasn't one of us.

"Man, I call fluke!" sneered Bray.

"Imma co-sign that!" Mikey said, laughing.

"Just you wait, fellas," I replied warmly. "Gimme a second to suit up. History'll repeat itself!"

"It damn sure won't," said a slurred, raspy voice. The crowd went silent. "Don't you dare try that dunk shit over here." I looked left and right to match voice to face and found emerging from the crowd a stocky mid-to-late-twenties hothead approaching. Around his neck was a silver chain with a nickel-sized pendant, inscribed with Roman numerals and a cherub in the middle. This guy took a swig of whatever was in the brown paper bag he was holding. "Betcha still can't get an offer, even with all that hype you got goin' on," he said. A whiff of the hard stuff escaped as he spoke. "Ain't that right, Simmy?"

"Yo, Jame. Chill out with all that," Simeon intervened. Little did I know he was also the centre of attention here after last week's game — but for mockery rather than praise.

"C'mon, Simmy. Lemme suit up and show this bozo what a real highlight's all about."

"You talk a whole lotta game, huh," I rebutted. "Watch it, you might be my next victim. Better hope no one pulls their phone out." Hisses echoed from the crowd. This *Jame* guy — with his boozy breath and drawstring bag strapped over his shoulders — he was straight-up fuming. He carefully took off his janky chain and widened the opening of his bag, gently placing it inside. What he gathered from the bag was a pair of worn-out high-tops.

And before I knew it, I was knee-deep into a best-of-three series. I thought I'd gotten myself into some ordinary pickup with meaningless trash talk, but oh, was I wrong. Because Jame would soon reveal his true motives.

* * *

By twilight, we neared the finale of game three. First team to eleven points wins, with a win-by-two rule. The score was 10–9, advantage: the kids from Oakwood with a familiar ally in Mikey. Simeon, alongside Bray (who would have been just as useful munching on popcorn from the sideline), and this *Jame* dude — whoever he was — were on the brink of defeat.

Game point.

I found myself squinting whenever I turned to the crowd, spotting dozens of phone lights illuminating the blacktop amid the looming darkness. But soon, I realized people were pulling out their phones to capture footage in case a fight broke out — and not a highlight — because this was no longer basketball. Hand checks became smacks and strikes to the gut. Tripping and shoving and any other malicious scheme took over.

"Check," I proposed. Jame flung the ball at my feet, but I held back from doing the same. He began pressing up on me, so I took a few jab steps to gain some real estate. Now, Jame was by no means a skilled ballplayer, but he somehow stood a chance. He had tortoise-like agility and lacked any sort of novice skill, but his cheap shots and scrappiness helped him stay in front of me whenever he did. With no referees and Jame's newfound home-court advantage, I was playing his game, and I had to figure out how to seal a win under his rules.

I dribbled a few times between my legs and behind my back, then pulled some crossovers to keep him guessing. He was slow on my fakes, so whenever I caught him off balance, he'd hear the hollers and gasps from his home crowd.

"Lock him up, Jame!" I heard as he shoved me out of stance. I took a strong dribble to the foul line and created some space, giving a pump fake and getting Jame to bite on it. I stepped around him, tossing the ball high off the backboard. And in spite of Jame smacking me hard on my arm, I still threw down an emphatic, game-winning flush.

"And ooooooooone!" I roared to the crowd.

Jame dragged himself to a near bench, scowling as he returned to his drawstring bag.

Keele hollered at me, "Damn, bro! Gamed 'em with the hoop *and* the harm! That's how you're feelin'?" He slapped me five as Mikey, Bray, and others swarmed.

Simeon approached. "Good game," he said, solemnly. I noticed Jame creeping from behind him, which I thought was a bit suspect.

"Good game, brotha" I replied.

I turned away from the crowd in search of the girl — the girl with the simple yet versatile hairdos who was two-for-two in being spotted before I'd do something spectacular. I was *it*. The man of the hour, once again. At least I thought I was.

Some muttering caught my attention, I assumed either from Simeon or Jame, though I couldn't quite distinguish between the two. "Watch out, Yoosie!" someone screeched. I swiftly turned and found Simeon; he shoved me away before I could react. The commotion had me oblivious and confused.

Shliiing!

The crowd froze.

I heard a loud clatter then saw a boxcutter flopping onto the cold tarmac, only to reveal it was Jame whose bloody fingers had held it. Jame's hands trembled; his breaths shallowed in fright. Simeon fell to his knees, then to the ground. Ear-splitting shrieks permeated the air.

A dark red stain seeped through Simeon's shirt, spreading from the site of the wound to the hemline. I saw bodies scatter from where he lay.

Then I saw her. There she was, looking for someone amid the terror but still floating above the chaos. She looked to her left, then to her right, then dead centre into the distance where I stood, shaken.

She slowly approached and looked me in my eyes, a frozen gaze at the panic that I felt on my face. I looked at her the same way. And despite the horror surrounding the two of us and the fleeing bodies that whipped past, nothing mattered but the speechless moment we shared.

For in that blink, I felt as though everything was okay and perfectly fine and that I was exactly where I needed to be.

Because I found her. The girl.

And she found me. Maureen.

CHAPTER VIII
UNANNOUNCED

PRESENT

It's curious how Feldbrook's so speechless.

He's just sitting there gaping at me, as though unpacking the trauma at Woolner Park should've been a topic left off the table. Okay, sure, maybe we've derailed from mulling over my troubles on the hardwood — but after all, that nightmarish episode *did* happen on a basketball court too, so it's all the same grief, I suppose. I mean, he had to have heard worse throughout his years.

I feel the tension thicken, hearing every tick of the clock behind him. Then finally, he builds up the nerve to ask me, "What ended up happening … to your friend?"

Feldbrook's nearly lost for words, and I understand

why. Because it's hitting me too: the shock, the terror, the fear from that night — I also find myself having not a single word to paint how I felt about it. How I *feel* about it.

I guess I must've blocked it out from my thoughts like it never happened (that's gotta be a brain response, having a trauma erased from my mind — some sort of amnesia or something, right?). Because up until now, I wouldn't have thought of what happened to Simeon if I wasn't lured into retelling my life story, lured into going back to that horrible Thursday.

"Udoka … you with me?" I hear Feldbrook snap his fingers.

"Oh! Umm … I'm — what was the question?"

"What happened to Simeon after that incident?"

"Right…" I sigh, finding myself drooping forward. I bet Feldbrook's staring at me, jotting down my discomfort in his notepad. "Simeon, he, umm…"

"It's okay," Feldbrook tells me softly, then asks if I can walk him through whatever I remember happening the next day, which is, strangely enough, still crystal-clear in my mind.

PAST

The next day, that eerie Friday, I left class and crept along the empty corridor trembling in my bones. The monotone announcement blaring out from the P.A. made everything a thousand times worse:

"Please excuse the interruption … Attention staff and students … Udoka Clendon, please come to Principal Keller's office … Udoka Clendon, immediately, thank you."

* * *

I stood by the etched glass window and saw the shadow of a tall figure wearing a peaked cap. The silhouette pulled open the door; I immediately noticed her badge and duty belt. Trouble awaited, and I knew it.

"You were at Woolner Park yesterday evening, weren't you, young man?" I felt beads of sweat trickling down my neck. I couldn't muster a response. "My son saw you as he was heading out, he was tellin' me."

"Oh," I said. "Did he?"

"He's always shootin' around over there. Y'know, before the *big kids* take over the court. He said there was a huge crowd. And all sorts of screaming and shouting and commotion after he started walking home. What happened?"

I hid my hands in my pockets as they began to tremble. "Uh … the, umm…"

The officer adjusted her duty belt. I continued stammering, staring at her handcuffs and steel baton. She glared at me suspiciously as I became more nervous.

"Well?"

"A dunk … a dunk happened."

"A dunk?"

I nodded.

"*Your* dunk?"

Again, I nodded.

"Another one, eh! You're number … number five on the team, if I'm not mistaken?"

Hesitantly, I dipped my head a third time.

"My son's a huge fan. Quite the compliment from a child," she teased, "but a fan's a fan. Helluva play you had last game." She swept through the main office door and was about to leave, but then she held it open as though she'd forgotten something. "Eh, Keller!" she shouted, her heel wedging the door ajar. "Don't forget — safety workshop, Monday afternoon! Tell your staff, tell your kids. Eh, even tell your staff to tell your kids!" The officer took her foot off the door and looked at me sternly, bowing her head as she left. "Keep it up, young man."

"Will do, Officer." *Phew.*

I politely knocked on the door, no longer leery but curious as to why I was called down. I thumped on it again. *Whatever happens, happens.*

"Come in."

"Principal Keller?"

"Yoosie," she said. "Grab a seat." Hanging from the wall behind her were grainy, black-and-white team portraits and dusty medals that I assumed came from her playing days. I gleaned she had been following Oakwood athletics; very few teachers or admins greeted me as *Yoosie*, which she must've picked up at our home games.

Also seated in Principal Keller's office was a middle-aged man, hunched over in his chair. He wore plain khakis and had his glasses tucked between the buttons of his collared shirt. He glanced at me several times, hoping I wouldn't notice, and seemed rather unsettled whenever I did. *Was he there last night? Does he know something I don't know?*

"This gentleman would like to have a word with you," said Principal Keller. "Sound all right, Yoosie?"

"Umm, sure."

"Wonderful! Would you prefer I stay, or should I step out for a moment?"

"Stay, Principal Keller. You can stay."

"I trust you're okay with this too, Coach?"

He eagerly nodded, all fidgety and nervous. *Wait, what was that? 'Coach'?* As in, a *Division 1 coach* who'd been scouting me all this while? A *Division 1 coach* who would offer me a full ride to *Wherever State University* by the end of this meet-and-greet? A *Division 1 coach* who would prove that the Hoopblog clip destined me for much more than my fifteen minutes of fame? It had reached a couple thousand hits by then, and I obsessed over the thought of it gaining more and more views from more and more people so I could garner the interest of some coach and land an offer or two before the hype would settle. I thought maybe, just maybe, this was my sixteenth minute. *Hi, Coach. Yoosie Clendon here. Upon which dotted line do I sign*?

He stood up while Principal Keller began introducing him, though I was caught trying to figure out who he was, let alone where he coached. He seemed remarkably familiar on second thought.

"So, Yoosie," said Principal Keller. "Coach here tells me he's kept an eye on you for quite some time."

"Yes, ma'am!" he interrupted. "For years."

"Well, Coach, it seems like Yoosie's spent many, many hours molding himself into the stellar scholar-athlete he is today. Without question, he'll be a star."

"Thank you, Principal Keller," I humbly responded.

The man peered at me again, probably studying my subtle mannerisms, observing my responses to flattery and how they'd translate to whether I'd be easy to coach, easy to instruct, willing to follow orders, that sort of thing. "Oh, definitely," he said. "In due time."

Wait, what'd he say?

I remained stuck on those three, strikingly peculiar words: *In due time … in due time … in due time*. The phrase had resonated with me some time ago, even if I couldn't put a finger on it. It had a distinct pitch and was spoken in the same tone as the man sitting before me. So, it *was* him. Yes, it was definitely him.

I'd seen this man before.

I'd *known* him.

But from where?

I sat staring at the blank ceiling, suddenly feeling disengaged. The conversation could've gone on just as it did, regardless of whether I was sitting with Principal Keller and this mysterious man. So, I began reminiscing about the summer evenings where I'd shoot hoops at Woolner Park as a kid, feeling a presence there with me. There must've been a voice. This man's voice, it felt like...

I remembered how I'd fantasize about playing on the biggest stages against the best in the game: "*Clendon's guarded by Kobe with seconds left ... the clock winds down as the crowd rises to its feet ... he fakes to his left, then to his right*," the voice would say.

"Two seconds left!" I'd shout in my child's high-pitched voice, pretending my novice moves were the polished shimmies of the pros on TV, visualizing people by the windows of surrounding apartment buildings like they were fans watching from the nosebleeds in this arena of my imagination...

"*Clendon fires...*" I'd hear. "*... And he scores! Clendon sinks it for the game! It's over! It's all over!*"

I'd prance and shout and pump my fists as though it were all real; as though this mystifying presence from my memory had instilled the belief that this was all possible. "That'll be you one day," it would say, "for real.

Never stop dreaming, Udoka."

"You ... you think so?" I would ask.

"*For real*, kiddo. It'll happen. *In due time,*" the voice would reply, fetching rebound after rebound.

Then it hit me.

The sound of this voice — resonating within that decorated office space — was impossible to confuse any longer. It was from none other than this fidgety man in the collared shirt...

"It's you!" I blurted out. "What are you doing here?"

Silence fell.

He turned toward me. "Udoka," he responded.

Principal Keller stopped and froze. She carefully set her eyes onto me, then him. The tension was unbearable. "Maybe I'll leave you two alone, after all," she said.

CHAPTER IX
ROAD TRIP

PRESENT

My chin rests on my palm, my elbow on the armrest. I now feel comfortable here. Liberated. At ease that the stories, the secrets, the feelings I spew out will all be secure within the vault of these four walls. No longer is Feldbrook just this bland psych prof who chats with me from time to time; nor do I think he still sees me as the damaged jock from one of the university's varsity teams that knocked on his door a while back. He has become someone I can trust. A confidant.

He follows me as I plunge into the abyss for my darkest thoughts, conjuring schemes for me to bring them to the surface as if they weren't secrets I've kept to myself all my life. With him, I feel comfortable talking about virtually anything, especially Pop — a touchy topic in and of itself.

"What did you think was the reason he visited your high school?" he asks. "I mean, you oughta be naïve or damn near born yesterday to think it was a coincidence that Pop just reappeared outta nowhere."

I stare at Feldbrook, puzzled. "How do you figure?"

"Well, wrap your head around it. He disappears without reason. *Poof*! Gone for years. Then you get your big break, and—"

"But it—"

"He *conveniently* comes back just a matter of days later," Feldbrook rambles, oblivious to the scowl I'm giving him. "He saw an opportunity, a way back in. *Congrats, son*! *What a play you had*! *Oh, and forgive my absence, but how've you been, by the way*?"

"It wasn't—"

"That big game of yours was his excuse to creep back into your life. It was the beginning of your would-be superstar career, he thought. I bet you were his meal ticket to a promising fortune."

"It wasn't like that!" My fist pummels his desk. I feel the ground shake, the air being sucked out of the room.

"So, then," he says, smirking, "what *was* it like?"

"Not *that*."

"Enlighten me."

"Well, first of all," I reply, trying to keep my calm, "*Pop*. He was no opportunist."

"How so?"

"There'd be no story to tell if not for him! Nothing!"

He shrugs. "Well—"

"No, Doc!" I interject. "Pop didn't '*reappear*' for my '*big break*,' or whatever you call it. There'd be no story. No highlight dunk on the 'net, no scholarship, and therefore no chance of me sitting in front of *you* — the psych at *this* fine institution, right here and right now, spilling my life story like it's any ordinary conversation — if not for him! None of this, none of it woulda been possible for me. He gave *me* the opportunity!"

I lean forward on the edge of my chair; Feldbrook is drawn back in his. "Sure," he says. "Okay."

"These opportunities wouldn't've existed had he stayed dormant, had he dismissed this little dream of mine, had he said, 'Nah, focus on something else, something more substantial.' And that blog. *Hah*! The craze came and went like the breeze past your nose on a cold, windy Toronto day. It brought me nothing but likes, follows, and views online. No recruitment, no coaches, no nothing. But who do you think was there after that, doing all he could to find me the next opportunity to reap what he felt I deserved?"

I glare at Feldbrook, awaiting his response.

He nods regretfully.

"Well?" I persist.

"My apology, kid. So really, then. Why'd Pop visit you unannounced?"

"It wasn't—"

"Better yet, what happened after that? What was that 'next opportunity?'"

I catch a glimpse of the time. It's well past twelve thirty, and I'm sure he knows it too. But he's overly invested in this past of mine. He wants to explore these memories, relive them with me, now, and not next session.

PAST

Nobody in their teens plays basketball for fun.

Let me repeat that: *nobody in their teens plays basketball for fun.*

I mean, *nobody* might be a stretch, but I don't think it is. Because there isn't anyone that I've come across past their adolescence who's told me basketball was "just a hobby" or "nothing but a fun game." Nope, not where I'm from. Never have I heard such blasphemy.

Because for me, at least, basketball was my life. Basketball was my nourishment. She was my heartbeat and my breath, the basis of many fantasies running through my mind during the quiet hours of the night. She was my promising vehicle to fame and riches for me and my future family. But above all those things, She was my passion; She was my love; She was my purpose.

She was the reason I found myself stooped by the windows of a crammed Greyhound during springtime. My sophomore season at Oakwood had just finished, and travel season was upon me — a golden opportunity to put my game on centre-stage in front of heaps of D-1 scouts and coaches; my chance to earn a full-ride scholarship, where I'd eventually put together a stellar career at whichever school, then live out my dream of playing in the big leagues.

First stop on the tour: Chicago, for an exposure camp.

He was there. With me. *For me.* Pop, that is, fast asleep in his cramped-up seat. I stared at him, thinking about the trip and what it meant to me, to him, to us; I revisited the blissful times we spent with just a ball and rickety hoop, years ago; I realized that basketball was what kept our relationship going but may have somehow, in some way, been the culprit in his absence from the family.

But enough with the melancholy. Pop — *he was there.*

He was there, flustered as he and I took on the foreign grid of the downtown Chicago streets, doing all he could to find us a place to stay that was remotely close to the venue.

He was there, perched on the narrow bleachers just like old times, marvelling over my polished jump shot and tight handles and how much my moves had improved since he'd taught me them. Pop was in awe of my growth from the skinny kid he once knew to the built fifteen-year-old he was witnessing.

He was there, gaping at my hops and midair spins that drew *oohs* and *aahs* from all corners of the gym and gave reason for me to join the dunk contest. I saw the thrill in his eyes, as though he was a kid in the stands who'd never seen a live dunk before. Because he hadn't seen *me* get up for a windmill jam or a 360-tomahawk flush before then. Not in person, at least.

He was there, rooting on his 6'1" underdog in the final round. "Jam it home!" he hollered, despite the times I'd arrived short at the rim on a dunk that seemed merely impossible. He still applauded me when the ball would clunk off the backside of the rim and ricochet to the rafters, even when he felt I'd jumped my highest. He still cheered tirelessly after I'd used up two attempts and was down to my last one.

I glanced at the basket, then at Pop, thinking about what went wrong on the pair of misses: I tossed the ball too far on the first try, too high on the second one. With both, though, I jumped a fraction of a second too late.

I caught a glimpse of the hoop once more, then took a shallow breath. Lobbing the ball perfectly this time, I anticipated its bounce at just an arm's length from the rim. Then, I leaped. I cradled the ball through my legs then swung it up and above my head, all the while twirling for a full spin. *This is it. This is the one.* I stretched and reached and hoped that She'd somehow make it over and through the hoop.

And She did.

Though as I tugged on the rim a jiff too long, the ball popped out from just beneath the basket and shot up into the air — and did not make it through the hoop after all. *Strike three.*

I frantically scanned the crowd for Pop as I landed. When I looked over my shoulder and found him with a consoling smirk, his arms crossed, and his shoulders shrugged as if to say, "better luck next time," I was put at ease noticing he was concealing his frustration, his disappointment, that typical stern look on his face. It was what made everything all right, at least for a moment.

Pop. *He was there.*

* * *

But there too was Pop, breaking the silence of midnight in the motel room. "Why the last dunk?"

"What ... what about it?"

"Why'd you try that one?"

"Why not?"

Pop rustled against his duvet and linens, and by the sound, I assumed he'd risen from his bed. "Well," he said, curt and snappy, "you didn't win."

"I tried, Pop."

"Tried?"

"Tried the hardest dunk I could think of," I explained. "What's wrong with that?"

"You ever pull it off before you *tried* it today?"

"Nah. Close. This one time at school," I replied. "But nah."

I heard a soft click by the nightstand between his bed and mine and was blinded by the lamp's glow. Pop — oh, surely — he was there, hovering over my bed as though it were an awful crime for me to lie fast asleep and dream about God knows what at two in the morning. He then asked, "Why do you play basketball?"

"What?"

"Why do you play basketball?"

I shielded my eyes from the lamp's glare in that dark, dark room, wondering for what dire reason I was wakened. He nudged my shoulder firmly, awaiting my reply, so I shouted, "I heard you, man!"

"So? Why do you play?"

"What's this about, Pop!"

"What do you mean, 'What's this about?' It's about you taking a second to think about what you're really doing here. What *I'm* really doing here. What you're aiming to get out of all of this. It's about answering a simple question, which I'll ask again," Pop said, without a breath in between his rant. "Why. Do you. Play basketball."

"What's going on, Pop! C'mon, man!" I yelled.

"Better yet, why's it the other way around?"

I kissed my teeth.

"Well?" he pressed. "Why's it somehow occur that basketball's playing you?" I was awfully confused, but I also had no idea how much this conversation would change my outlook. I'll never forget what Pop said next:

"Look at where we are. The other kids in that gym today came here in their family minivans. They slept in decent hotels. They woke up to a continental breakfast and stepped on the court fuelled up and ready to go. Now, look at you, man. Look at me. Look at us. How we got here. From the Greyhound to the train to the transit bus. Lugging our suitcases from block to block, looking for some cheap dinner and breakfast for the morning. Settling in late last night in this dusty old motel room. I scraped together all that I could to get you here, to provide you with this opportunity. So don't waste it, man! Play this game; don't let it play *you*. Use this game; don't let it use *you*. That dunk contest trophy coulda been right here on this creaky nightstand, shining so bright, we wouldn't've even needed a lamp for this place! Listen here. These coaches, these scouts, they don't care about how pretty your shot looks. They wanna know if it goes *in*! They don't care about your flashy jukes and dribbles and spins. They wanna know if you can get past the man guarding you! They don't care if you can loop the ball between your legs, once, twice, even three times before a dunk. They wanna know if you can slam it in the hoop!"

"All right! I get—"

"You *don't* get it!" he exclaimed. "Now, you can be ambitious and try your luck with a dunk you've never pulled off before, in front of all those people, but I can promise you no one'll remember a lick about who you were or what you did by next week. Because you couldn't pull through! You *lost*! People don't remember the runner-up. Coach or no coach, scout or no scout — people don't give a shit about losers!"

I groaned. "It's just a dunk comp—"

"It's not just a dunk competition! It trickles down to the shots you miss, the games you lose, the opportunities you let pass by. You get a chance to show what you're made of — don't waste it! Don't fall victim to this game, carrying on all cool and cocky and living out your glories in your thirties in some mediocre men's league against a bunch of washed-up scrubs 'cause you couldn't do it now when it mattered. Don't be that sorry has-been fifteen, twenty years from now that says, 'I almost won that dunk-off. I almost played for that coach at that school. I almost made it.' Almost, almost, almost!" he yelled. "If you tried something with the same flair and finesse, but just safer — you woulda got it done.

Something you had already practiced — you woulda got it done. Trying something you were sure of woulda got you that tall, shiny trophy and perhaps a coach or two writing up a letter a week from now about 'that Canadian kid' who had just what it took to show out in front of all those people. You never know! It's not just the dunk competition — it's the game of life; and this *game* could be yours for the taking, Udoka! Don't you see?" His voice softened. "*Use* basketball. Don't let it use you."

On my twin-sized cot I lay silent and motionless. Pop's sentiments began to resonate. He was there, delivering another cold slice of tough love. His words echoed for years in my head; for my benefit or not, I guess that's still in question.

But what was certain: Pop cared a great deal and did anything and everything he could to get me wherever he thought I could go.

He. Was. There.

He was there for New York, when he silenced his growling stomach so that I had something to snack on and wasn't hungry or parched before my final game.

He was there for Virginia, when he got us onto the local transit bus with the bottom quarters in his pockets, from our cruddy motel room to the glossy front doors of some big-time school's state-of-the-art arena.

He was there for Pittsburgh. For the tournaments in Detroit and Connecticut, too.

To the other side of the universe and back.

He was there. With me. *For me.* To no surprise.

CHAPTER X

WHEN I'M GONE

PAST

Leena lay sprawled on my bed, twiddling her feet in the air, aimlessly swiping her thumbs over my phone's screen. I had scavenged all the nooks in my bedroom for whatever I felt I should bring — a jumble of sneakers and comfy clothes; blankets I hadn't yet unfurled but suspected would be awfully useful come wintertime; booklets and pens and the petty school essentials that came to mind — I shoved them all into some old duffle bags and suitcases.

I found mementos that brought me back to where this journey began: from underneath my nightstand, a linty photograph of me holding on to Her in my puny arms, with Pop hoisting my then forty-pound body above his shoulders amid an autumn scene; cramped between old shoeboxes, a dusty diary booklet from a third-grade English project that told the story of eight-year-old me:

Dear diary,

On Saturday I scored 711 points on the basketball hoop at the park counting by 1s! If I was counting by 2s, it would be 1,422 points!

Sincerely,

Udoka

I knelt in front of my closet, overcome by nostalgia. Skimming through the pages, I was certain to find a passage from when Pop was there with me, witnessing the earliest stages of what would become my bitter love story:

Dear diary,

Yesterday me and Pop played a basketball game called 21. I won three games, Pop won one game. After that we played catch. I had lots of fun.

Sincerely,

Udoka

I even found — tucked in my sock drawer, seemingly to be rediscovered — player reports from my old rep coach, Coach Quinn. Like the one that read, *Clendon: Soft. Never says anything. Gets nervous and folds under pressure*; or the one from the following season, which had Lacks confidence in bold writing.

I would ruminate on those two words. They used to jump off the page and scream at me. Torment me. Follow me like a thick shadow. So I stared at them, glared at them, thinking then and there how I managed to somehow save face with that critique — by winning and making highlight plays and throwing down blog-worthy dunks and having Coach Quinn eventually share how proud and fond of me he had become. But I felt there was something hard to ignore that I'd be sweeping under the rug. The broom: admission into a fancy prep school in the U.S., where I could boast about finally getting that "top-tier" exposure I'd always wanted — I was graduating from Coach Quinn's opinion and on my way to play south of the border, the "real deal."

I wonder why I ignored those two bold words at first, as though my lack of confidence wasn't a deep-rooted issue to begin with. Because I was wrong. *It sure was.*

"Are you done yet?" asked Leena in her super-squeaky, inquisitive, twelve-year-old voice.

"I could ask the same," I replied. "What're you doing on that thing anyway?"

"Games. What else?"

"Don't you play enough of those?"

"I could ask *you* the same!" she parroted.

"Nope. Going far, far away to play some more games."

Leena rolled her eyes.

That spring, Leena would grow accustomed to me packing my things and heading across the land, one weekend at a time. Meanwhile, I'd enter American soil — New York, Virginia and so on — not knowing I'd return home empty-handed, as far as Division 1 offers or interests were concerned. Though not *every* trip was taken in vain, because the first one wasn't. After all, it turned out to be my showing in Chicago that had caught Coach Methers's eye.

* * *

I still remember the first time I spoke to him.

I was caught by surprise receiving a call from a number with an area code I'd never seen before. Although suspicious, I answered anyway, learning the caller was a "Coach Ellison Methers" who had apparently watched my dunks and crossovers and jump shots from the floor seats of that multi-gym facility — all of the same dunks and crossovers and jump shots that Pop had scrutinized and downplayed in that grubby motel room. Coach Methers saw something in my game; I don't know what it was, but his belief in me was the hope that I had needed. He seemed thrilled to iron out all the details of his program at Carinci Preparatory Academy, in Illinois — some hundred miles away from home, where the winters were, by some anomaly, just as brutal as Toronto's chilling temperatures and gusting winds.

"Our main floor leader's off to play in the Ivy League next year, so we'll need a young talent like you to buckle up and put 'er in full throttle! Someone who can lead us to the promised land," he said, the phone muffling his voice. "You willing to grab the keys, son?"

"Yes, Coach," I responded.

"I'd hope to have you visit campus sooner than later. Would love to show you around. Visit the library, the gym, our locker room. Meet the guys and all," he said, clearing his throat. "We'd love to have you on board, Udoka. At Carinci, you'll be the leader I'm sure you're capable of becoming."

What brought me on board must've been the sternness in his voice, the conviction in his tone, the future that he foresaw for me, and the utter belief that he meant everything he said. I mean, Oakwood had my heart, but it's no secret there's been better traction for Canadian players heading to the States in hopes of fulfilling their hoop dreams. And I had imagined that leaving Toronto for school seemed daunting, frightening, like something I hadn't ever done before, but I couldn't stay. The prospect of playing for Carinci Prep in the coming junior year seemed impossible to refuse.

* * *

I sat down by my closet door; Leena and I locked eyes.

"You gonna wish me safe travels before I leave?" I asked.

"Hmm ... lemme think..." She pressed a finger to her mouth, pondering dramatically. "Nope! You excited for *Ill-i-noise,* though?"

"*Illinois*, lil' sis. The 's' is silent."

"Uh-huh. Yeah, whatever."

"*What-ever*!" I mocked in her same super-squeaky, inquisitive, twelve-year-old voice. "And yeah, I'm ready. Just visiting there for now, though."

The doorbell suddenly rang — once, then repeatedly. Startled, Leena and I angled our ears downstairs, where we expected Ma to answer the door.

"Ella?" I asked Leena.

"Nuh-uh. Wonder who."

"How're you two doing, by the way? On TV yet?"

Leena became despondent, taking a moment to respond. "Well, yeah. *She* is."

"And you?"

"Not me. Kinda messed up my lines in the last audition," she admitted in a faint murmur.

Instantly, I witnessed a cloud of misery linger over her that seemed too heavy for any twelve-year-old to endure. Because she had a good feeling about this gig. Despite her alleged blunder, she came home the evening of the audition as confident as always, waiting by the kitchen phone for the call that would confirm she landed the role.

Leena obsessed over the performing arts, chasing her dream just as I did mine. She'd sit alone by the family TV, all enthused to watch reruns of her favourite sitcoms and mimic the dialogue, timely and by the syllable, just so she could practice what it'd be like to recite her own lines for some play or commercial or movie. She'd even rehearse the moves from pop music videos, strutting her stuff like the lead singer in front of a team of backup dancers — no matter how silly it seemed.

And that might've been the difference between us — she didn't care how silly she looked, or how far-fetched or delusional her dream might've been. *Heck,* I'd surely be telling an entirely different version of my story had I adopted her bold, fearless traits. She understood at a young age that her dream was *her* dream — *hers*, not anyone else's — which endowed her with an unshakeable confidence, an unapologetic pursuit of becoming whoever she wanted to be.

Weeks after her audition, I'd often catch a glimpse of Leena cross-armed and slouched on a dining chair, staring at the phone on the cluttered countertop. Quiet and still and consumed in her loneliness, she seemed unbothered by my concern for how long she was dragging herself through a disappointment she wasn't ready to face. "They're gonna call!" she'd shout, shooing me and my pessimism away. She'd wait and wait until her hope started to dwindle, until the day came when she figured that the telephone wasn't going to ring.

It was a grief she wouldn't accept but one she'd need to; a grief that would ignite her tenacity, her burning desire to reach her dreams.

Soon, that dining chair became vacant, as it should've been much earlier. Because Leena picked herself up and returned to the family TV, where she resumed reciting the dialogues and moves that she studied so thoroughly, envisioning again that one day she'd shine on that screen.

She was resilient beyond her years. Leena was down then, but surely not out.

* * *

"There'll be another one, right? Another gig?" I asked. Leena didn't reply but looked vacantly across my room instead. "Right?"

"What are those?" she asked, pointing her chin at a stack of envelopes under my dresser, fixating particularly on the few poking through the bottom drawers.

"Those? Oh. Nothing, really."

"Letters, it seems," she speculated.

"Something like that."

"From someone … important?"

"Mhm," I murmured.

"Like maybe," she puckered her lips to make kissy sounds, "love letters?"

"Nope."

"Who's the girl?"

"They're not that, Leena."

"Is she pretty? Tall? Would she like me?"

"They're not to or from any girl, Leena."

"What's her name!"

I replied, "There is no g—" but as I was firing back, barging through my door, looking frightened and out of breath, was… "Mo?"

"Mo?" questioned Leena. "Is this the girl?"

"What girl?" said Mo.

"The girl in my brother's letters!"

"Wait, what letters?" asked Mo. She turned and cut her eyes at me. "Who's the girl in your letters!"

I asked, "What are you doing here?"

Mo fluttered and fanned her face, mustering the composure to explain herself. "The park," she said, breathing heavily. "It was … it was at the park. Woolner Park."

"What was there?"

Tears began streaming down Mo's cheeks as she stood by the door, shaking, as though her thoughts had fallen into a rabbit hole of the worst outcomes imaginable.

"It was the last place ... the last place he told me he was headed."

CHAPTER XI

NEW KICKS, SORE FEET

PRESENT

Mo's face glimmers on my phone. Flashing on the screen is that silly selfie she took some time ago and saved as her caller profile — that goofy, gaping grin and flared nose thing she does. It usually reminds me that it's okay to lighten up before taking her calls. After all, I find joy in hearing her happily yap on about nothing special. But not this time. I won't acknowledge any of it. Because I know what she wants to say, what she wants to tell me.

Maybe blowing up my phone is how she deals with this gloomy, closed-off side of me: my one-word texts and the calls I've ignored; the desire to be left alone and distant from the mere thought of basketball. She saw this side of me a while back, but here it is again — my self-pity, my low spirits, after a crummy, underachieving freshman year playing university ball.

I stare at the bright screen. My phone rings once, twice, a third time — until it doesn't. I'm not for it, her solace and coddling. Because I'm outside of Feldbrook's office, ready for my weekly fix of his coddle-free time and attention.

His door swings open and smacks against the wall as a livid student storms out. "Apologies!" he shouts from his desk. "Whiny students and their sorry midterm grades, begging for a bump-up. Come on in." He quickly clears his desk. "Where'd we leave off?"

"Prep school."

"Yes! Right, yes. Where, again? I mean, right after Oakwood."

"Carinci Prep."

"Carinci, yes. Let's talk Carinci hoops. Take me there. First game that comes to mind, maybe?"

"Well, there was this one game..."

PAST

We took on Hayden Preparatory School for our home opener. There weren't many schools in our conference, so since we were well acquainted with Hayden and the other teams, each game had a rivalry-like feel. We'd known the tendencies of all the players on each team, right down the roster.

And on gamedays, in the stands of any gym was a wild student body prepped with their *own* game plans. They'd dig up any and every scandal they could find to throw an opponent off his game — which seemed gimmicky at first, but if tormenting the visitors into game-changing slip-ups was enough to squeeze out a win, then I guess the home fans did their part.

* * *

Anyway, Hayden held the advantage midway through the first quarter. With help from a 17–6 start to the game and early foul trouble for some of our key guys, our lively crowd was quickly silenced.

An irate Coach Methers paced along our bench, his arms clutched around his clipboard, stroking his chin whenever he looked my way.

"Clendon. Get Ron," he ordered. "Make a friggin' play out there!"

I nodded then dashed to the scorer's table, slipping out of my warm-up shirt. I could feel my heart thumping, witnessing diving bodies thudding against the floor and scuffing the hardwood's shiny polish. That's not to say I hadn't ever seen a loose-ball scramble before — I mean,

I've tussled for the ball a thousand times — but this, this felt different.

This game that I've known my entire life — more than I thought I'd known myself — suddenly seemed so unfamiliar, so foreign, so scenic. I felt the bright lights shining from all angles of the gym. The whistles screeching loudly over the fans and their ear-splitting roars. The frantic, back-and-forth pace of the game. The coaches' tantrums after a blown defense or unfavourable call, how they'd bellow from the depths of their lungs like their lives depended on a win, because in reality, their jobs very much might have. The sole realization that I, with so much to prove, could crumble at any given moment if I didn't "make a friggin' play" — I felt it all.

Speaking of blown defenses, Methers had spent heaps of time in practice over that past week harping on all sorts of schemes to stop Hayden from scoring. "Switch the high ball screens, force 'em left! Switch the high ball screens, force 'em left!" he shrieked in our empty gym at the crack of dawn until his lungs ached and our ears bled.

Methers was keen on our forwards switching onto Hayden's guards to block off their right lane, probably because they weren't great at making decisions going left. And since his scheme would force Hayden into throwing awkward lefty passes outside to the perimeter, anything less than a steal or turnover coming from every pick-and-roll was deemed a botched assignment.

This defense wasn't only practiced, it was engrained into my head and impossible to forget, such that Methers would have a fit if the coverage were blown. Simple strategy, of course, but with just moments before checking in, the concept eluded me.

The buzzer sounded and welcomed the substitutions. Sweat ran down my forehead as I stepped into the fire. I took a deep breath and told myself: *You got this*.

I sprinted down the court after inbounding the ball as Methers called a play from the sideline: "Swivel! Swivel!" I screened for Artie to clear some real estate for his post-up, then I set another pick for Ron before spacing behind the perimeter, waiting for a shot off a kick-out. I wasn't a main option for any of our plays, but it didn't cramp my effort on the court. After all, I was still new to the offense and hadn't gelled with it just yet, and there were stripes to be earned before becoming *the* go-to-guy.

* * *

We ran Swivel for the last few possessions to end the first half because Hayden couldn't stop any of our reads. Artie got a couple easy baskets inside, and Ron scored on a baseline jumper off the series of screens set for him. I got a couple touches here and there, but I hadn't even thought of looking at the basket to make a play for myself.

Hayden was bigger than us, quicker than us, and they relied on brute force to compensate for any lacking skill. My check was Arlotte Carmichael, Hayden's graduating PG, heading to play in the Big Ten for that following year. The differences between him and me were what seemed a thirty-pound size advantage in his favour, a few All-State honours, and the ability to read the floor over my head with his six-foot-six stature. He carried a well-balanced arsenal of finesse and strength: his fakes and elusive spins kept me on my toes for his next move, but he also had broad shoulders willing to poke at my chin should I dare reach at his dribble, and the power to plough his way to the basket at will.

Initially, he pressed me whenever I caught the ball and bullied me down the floor every chance he could, but I knew I had to fend for myself despite my disadvantages. Because as soon as I had subbed in, I was tested against a whole 'nother level of the game, a level to which I hadn't often been exposed back home: punishing, unrelenting physicality — during every running second, at any position.

So when Carmichael pushed, I learned I had no choice but push back harder. When a rebound was up for grabs, I threw my body in front of him and made sure he felt I was there. When he fought to get open along the perimeter, there I was, tugging at his jersey and disrupting every pass coming his way.

We held an eleven-point advantage before the final

play leading into halftime.

Since their early lead, Hayden didn't have much going for them offensively. Every sideline catch was double-teamed, and there was a rotation waiting to intercept their next pass wherever the ball went. Scoring off one-on-ones was their only hope to keep the game close. To my plight, it was none other than Carmichael who had just begun heating up, scoring Hayden's last three baskets on me and me alone, pinpointing me as the culprit for our diminishing lead.

Carmichael held the ball for the last shot of the half. He glanced at the flickering scoreboard as seconds wound down. I glowered into his eyes as though to say, *Nothing but a freight train will get past me this time.* He called for a ball screen at the top of the arc, expecting Artie to switch onto him for a mismatch. To his surprise, I fought over the screen and remained his check. So far in our matchup, it was apparent he had the upper hand, but I refused to shy away.

"Switch! Where's the ... where the hell's the goddamn switch!" screeched a baffled Methers. I smacked the hardwood and took my low stance before Carmichael. *Don't let him go right ... don't let him go right.*

Five seconds 'til halftime.

He jabbed to his right, though I didn't react, so I pressed into his hip to give a few honest swipes at the ball. *Don't let him go right*! He dribbled behind his back once, then twice, then between his legs a few times, until I shuffled back to my heels. Carmichael stutter-stepped to his left, then crossed over to his right, slicing past my body and into the lane. Artie approached as the help defense, but he was too late. So, Carmichael wrapped the ball across his waist and scooped it under Artie's reach to have it gently kiss the glass. The ball dropped into the hoop, grazing nothing but net.

We ended the first half leading 43–34.

Artie shoved my shoulder. "Stick to the game plan, man!" he yelled. "I had Carmichael!"

* * *

I sat slouched on the locker room floor, my head buried in my arms. I overheard Methers in the hallway before he entered, shouting, "Clendon can't guard a soul! Not a friggin' soul!"

To my left was Ron, who surely heard Methers too. "Shake it off," he whispered as the coaches entered. "You got another half."

Methers continued rambling, now without any effort to be discreet. "Why do we prep hours of film if you guys can't stick to a game plan! Forget a game plan, we can't even stick to our damn matchups! If you can't defend, you can't play — simple! Watch from the stands! Hell, don't even show up!" He knelt in front of me. "Am I clear?"

I nodded, sinking my head deeper between my shoulders.

"Not a friggin' soul," he muttered again, marking the chalkboard with X's and O's and second-half strategies that all but escaped the orbit of my troubled mind.

Ron nudged me. *You got this*, he mouthed.

Methers subbed me in for the second half a few times, but mentally I'd checked out of the game for good. We surmounted a strong third quarter lead that carried into the fourth and won by a double-digit margin.

But scarce were the reasons for me to celebrate.

PRESENT

"That Methers coach meant no harm, kid," Feldbrook assures me. "Why were you so thrown off your game?"

"His antics didn't bother me. Not then, not ever. I knew what I signed up for," I respond firmly, with no intention of playing the victim. Methers was strict, sure. But in no way was he tyrannical. He paid the utmost respect to his team by pushing everyone to what he thought was their brink of excellence, and then some. His philosophy involved squeezing every ounce of potential from his players for the sake of evolving them, growing them, developing them into polished individuals on and off the court. So much so that he felt cutting some slack was not only a disservice to that player, but also to the team. "A couple cusses didn't shake me," I reiterate.

"Then what did?" Feldbrook asks. "Was it your screw-up of that defensive scheme, or whatever?"

Hesitant to respond, I tell him, "The more I thought about not screwing up, the more it happened. You're a doctor, right? What's the science behind that?"

"Hmm," Feldbrook murmurs, resting one foot atop his other thigh. "I was like you some time ago. Underachieving college shortstop. I'd gotten everything I wanted from baseball, until one day I blinked and realized it was all different. Couldn't hit a ball if it were melon-sized and couldn't fetch one even if it was rolled right to me. But if only I knew back then what I know now..."

"What changed?"

Feldbrook shrugs. "What changed with *you*?"

I shrug back.

"Exactly. You never really know. It's why I study this discipline. I wanted to know what was happening inside my head thirty years ago when I was some pounds lighter and my hair was all pepper, no salt. I wanted to know what frame of mind I should've had. Not so I can turn back time and make amends with the pitches that missed my bat or the fly balls that missed my glove — because I can't go back — but so I can help folks like you. To give some insight on what I'd be thinking if I were in your situations."

"Take me there," I reply. "Anywhere. What would you

have done differently?"

"I would've focused on having fun."

"Fun." *That's not vague at all, Doc. I should jot that down before I forget it: F-U-N.*

"Yeah, *fun.*" He crosses his arms like he's about to follow that with a rundown. "Because it's easy to forget the reason you started playing to begin with. Kid, I'll tell you … I was a nervous wreck out on that field. I used to dread messing up. I'd put all this unnecessary pressure on myself — and for what? That pressure was distracting — it sucked the fun outta baseball and killed my game in the process. My head wasn't clear, which made me lose sight of why I was playing. I should've embraced striking out. I should've embraced being unable to field the ball. I should've been so deeply caught in the thrill of playing to the point where the pressures and mistakes didn't matter. I should've brushed it all off and continued having *fun,* believing that I'd redeem myself on the next play, or the next play after that." He sighs. "But this isn't about me. I assume you asked wanting to know what *you* should do differently."

"Mhm."

"Well, for starters, don't make the moment bigger than it is! The goal's to bounce a ball down a hardwood floor and toss it into a cylinder — it shouldn't be on a do-or-die pedestal! Performing a surgery, landing a plane — that's pressure. Not sports!" I'm musing at Feldbrook's points. I never thought of basketball from this perspective. "Who cares if you let so-and-so dribble to his right. Hustle back and stuff his shot anyway!"

"Carmichael."

"Yeah, him. Whoever. Lemme ask you this — if you had another crack at it, how would you guard him differently?"

"I'd keep him from going right." Feldbrook's giving me this blank stare. "By angling myself to the—"

"Wrong!" he shouts. "Well, sure, but wrong idea."

I shrug, feeling flustered. "Beats me, then."

"Two things. One — trying to steer clear of making the same mistake is like attracting it to happen again, because you're still thinking about it. By dwelling on what's-his-name dribbling to his right, you're still giving that negative outcome attention. Focusing on not repeating that mistake might cause it to unfold another time."

"Not quite following..."

"You ever miss a shot so badly because you were caught thinking about clanking one from before?" I'm slow to respond, still trying to make sense of this, but it seems like Feldbrook knows he's getting to me. "Thinking of the error could cause it to reoccur. Got it?"

"Okay. Yeah."

"And my second point — trying to avoid mistakes can distract you from the game's objective. Think about it — what was your old coach's endgame with that strategy?"

I'm bound to respond with something stupid; it's like

Feldbrook has his hand hovering over a 'wrong answer' buzzer. But I guess that's just it: whatever had been going on in my head wasn't right.

"To force Hayden … into awkward, lefty passes…"

"All wrong!" he shouts. "It was to keep them from scoring, you forget? Because even if you kept your man from dribbling to where he wants to go, but still gave up a basket, that wouldn't've pleased your coach, right?"

"Guess not."

"How about thinking, 'I'm gonna keep him from getting to the basket this time!' instead of, 'Don't let him dribble right, I'll get benched.' Why not try, 'I'm gonna sink my next shot,' and not, 'I better not miss this one!'"

"Hmm. All right."

"Don't let a mistake tamper with your game, kid. Fretting about a past mistake keeps you from competing, from reaching your true potential, from playing your game and having fun out there! Don't think, just play!"

"Just have fun, you say?"

Feldbrook nods.

"That'll get me benched, too! I can't just run around and do my own thing. What about the game plan?"

"Be in the moment. Worrying about what'll come if you mess up the strategy — that's distracting, that's not fun. Your mind wasn't where it needed to be. Your body was there on that court, slapping the floor before you played D, but *you* — you weren't present."

"So what are you saying?" I ask him. "How could I have been present?"

"Be in the moment, like I said. Stay mindful of the strategy. But be *there*, on the court, taking on ... what's his name?"

"Carmichael!"

"Yeah, whoever. Enjoy the challenge of guarding him even after he scored a few on you. Worrying about how or why he got a basket on the previous play, or even the ones before then — that's you, focusing on the past. Worrying about getting chewed out at halftime because of your defense — that's you, contemplating the future."

Bzzz! Bzzz!

I slouch to slip out my phone.

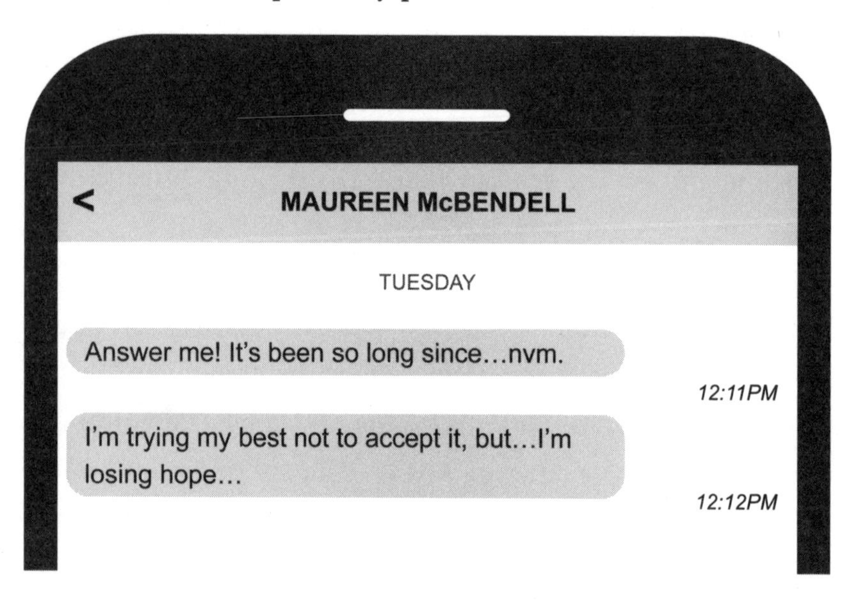

I'm flushed with remorse having forgotten she's caught in her own distress.

"Udoka?" I hear Feldbrook snap his fingers. "Udoka, do you understand?"

"Yeah, yeah, I'm here, Doc. I'm here."

"No, you're not. You're on your phone. Be *present*!"

CHAPTER XII

K[NO]W SACRIFICE, K[NO]W GLORY

PAST

Junior year was a write-off. And that's *write-off* described in the kindest, most pleasant of terms. I mean, despite the crucial screw-ups, the pressure to "make an [insert-expletive-here] play," the several times I had my ears rung off by many other people than Methers — my eleventh-grade season with Carinci Prep was still irreparable. And that's not even to mention the elbow that flung into my face and broke my nose during a tussle for a rebound, or the torn ligaments in my thumb and ankle, or my playing time that diminished along with my self-confidence — because ultimately, even if none of those things ever happened, junior year was written off because I began to lose my *feel* for the game, which was most difficult to handle.

In the offseason before a clean-slate senior year, I spent my mornings, afternoons, and nights in the gym, on the track, or in the weight room, hoping to rekindle the connection to Her that I was losing.

It would've been easier returning home for that summer. It would've been easier reverting to the raw competition that Woolner Park's pickup runs had to offer; it might've revived my dying spirit and ego.

Home. Oh, how practical that could've been. But *practical* wouldn't've helped me.

During those early summer mornings, I thought a productive offseason would allow me to save face for the coming fall — a chance for me to make up for every weak facet of my game. So, I had to stay on campus. Ron was here. Artie and a few others were, too. And whatever they'd been doing to improve, I wanted the same for me, and then some. It was a no-brainer.

* * *

Dripping with sweat, I'd hunch over with my hands pressed to my knees, pondering what I could do to instil a confidence like Ron's or a mentality as fearless as Artie's. I'd thought if I could exceed their effort, their output, their productivity in those several weeks, then my work ethic would iron out my worries altogether. So I aimed to outrun them in the footraces, outshoot them in the shooting drills, outlift them in the workouts, and outplay them in the scrimmages — all this I hoped would shrink the gap between me and two of the team's "go-to guys."

I lived up to those expectations as much as I could, though at times I was unable to surmount Ron and Artie. And coming up short — against either of them or anyone else in the training — brought out a fury that I had to conceal and channel into motivation.

So, whatever Ron's fastest mile was, I felt an urge to cross the finish line a few seconds sooner. Regardless of how many threes Artie would score in a minute, I needed to top that by at least a couple baskets. If they benched ten reps, I made it my mission to press eleven, at minimum. I figured this was the only way I'd climb the totem pole come September of senior year.

And it worked. I did.

But for the first time ever, I saw Her not as my first true love but as this insatiable presence in my mind that just wanted more and more from me whenever I felt I had been outdone on the court. I searched within for an unrelenting competitive edge to fuel me when I was exhausted. It distracted me from the fatigue; I was numb to the soreness, the pain. I silenced the voice in my head pleading to ease off the gas pedal, the voice begging I pump the brakes and reflect on the process.

Plodding toward the bathroom sink at early-morning hours, my eyelids heavy and puffy and battling to stay open, I would stare into the mirror and see nothing. Feel nothing. Feel empty and less than whole, because the gratification I had sought from day one of the offseason, the joy of the game I had yearned for — these were absent. I'd stare at this composition of sore, heavy muscles and stiff limbs and wonder why I hadn't relished the grind or embraced the sacrifice like I should have. I didn't have a chance to think about it all; a 6:00 a.m. workout was some fifteen minutes away. Basketball became a maddening obsession, a burdening chore with little purpose. I'd lost myself, completely.

PRESENT

"And how'd that year go for you?" Feldbrook asks. "That *clean-slate* senior year."

"Good," I say with a shrug. "For a while."

"*For a while...*" he muses. "Why only *a while*?"

"We were winning. My minutes were up. I mean, I was starting, even. Peak of my game, all that. Finally proving to Methers, to my teammates, to *everyone,* that I could play at the level expected of me."

Feldbrook stares at me. "But?"

"But then some games into the season, I took a blow to the head. Thought it was nothing. But nope. Concussed and sidelined for the next six weeks. I couldn't play. Couldn't practice. Man, I could hardly tolerate watching a ball bounce or hearing a whistle blow without wearing sunglasses and earplugs."

"That's unfortunate, really. But try again, though," Feldbrook says, with a stern look that suggests I think harder, dig deeper.

"But *what*?"

"Like you said, the season was 'good for a while.' But despite the concussion, why else wasn't the 'good' sustained?"

"No clue."

"Basketball, your newfound 'maddening obsession,' your 'burdening chore,' you say. Why—"

"Why *what*?"

"Why did the one aspect of your life, that used to make you feel on top of the world, turn into a chore? You lost something. What did you lose?"

"Fun, enjoyment. I don't know."

"Uh-huh. Well, I suppose. But you lost more than that."

"Sleep?"

"C'mon, Udoka. You said it about a minute ago."

"My purpose?"

"Your *purpose*!" Feldbrook exclaims. "You gave me this elaborate Rocky Balboa coming-of-age story in describing your offseason regimen. I practically heard

'Getting Strong Now' playing in my head. You worked and worked until it robbed you of your joy."

"That's what that song's called?"

"Focus! You mentioned this whole plan to be better than Ron and Artie and the rest of your teammates, but what you forgot was your *purpose* that began your whole story. It was your *feel* for the game that you lost. Your *passion*, remember?"

"So, you're saying I should've focused on regaining those things that summer?"

"What I'm saying is your senior year might've only been good 'for a while,' not because you got concussed, but because you lost your purpose, your reason, your 'why!' Being better than Ron or Artie couldn't've instilled purpose in you. It shouldn't've."

"Hmm..."

"Look, you worked your ass off trying to be better than everyone else. It drained you. Why was that your benchmark for a useful offseason? And why wasn't it measured by how good you were on the first day of training versus the last day, or how you felt about yourself before and after?"

"Isn't that the purpose of sports? To compete? To be the better player?"

"On paper, sure. On the scoreboard, most definitely," he says. "But deep down, that's not real. My true purpose on the diamond was becoming better than the player I was the day before. Becoming better than the *person* I was the day before. For me, it became about growing, evolving. And it helped my game after struggling for so long. There was passion in that. There was purpose there. Achieving that meant something to me in only a way that I understood. And I think finding your purpose could help you too. Not for your teammates, your coaches. Not even for Pop. For *you*."

"Now, how do *you* figure that, Doc?"

Feldbrook peeks over at me. He cracks a smile as though he'd been longing for this conversation...

FELDBROOK'S LESSON

Win from within. Be a better you; focus on a better you. Compete with a previous version of yourself and aspire to surpass it — again and again. Race against yourself and aim to beat your own timed mile, and if you're a bit slow, try again until your lungs cry. Aspire to raise your own bar; be stronger than yesterday's you.

Competing against opponents when the game is on is, obviously, ideal. But when the seats are empty and the lights are dim, when the goal is to improve *yourself*, do just that. This strategy is more useful because you know your abilities better than someone else's, and shrinking the gap between who you are and who you want to become is easier to gauge than a gap between you and another person. Throughout the process, competing against yourself may become more measurable, personal, fulfilling, and ultimately more purposeful.

We haven't been taught to celebrate the silver medals, or the efforts undeserving of *any* hardware in the trophy case. Instead, we celebrate the champion only; we subscribe to the 'win at all costs' mantra. Not at all is the traditional 'winning' attitude flawed; but it's important to consider that a winning attitude is not just the victor's. It is not the greater number on the scoreboard, or the fastest time, or even the most made baskets that should define 'winning.' What should is a pursuit of your own excellence; a drive to compete enthusiastically, passionately; an appetite for evolving yourself and becoming the best that you can be.

Don't focus on the end result of a competition, but on the process of bettering yourself, because if a gold medal or shiny trophy is all that keeps you going, then you'll depend on that to validate your strengths and efforts. And in the event you fall short of 'winning,' you might question your skillset, your efficacy, your *self*.

But when you're your own competition, there's no limit to what you can achieve.

What matters is how you perceive *your* reality. *What is real to you? What isn't?* Think about winning and what it means to *you*, because what matters is what *you* believe are the winning qualities of a person, and how these qualities compare to your own self. Is the Venn diagram separated, or is there overlap? And if there is, how much? Does this make you a winner? Are *you* a winner? *Why*?

* * *

After he's said his piece, I can't help but shrug. "I … dunno."

"You dunno?" Feldbrook crosses his legs and sighs sarcastically. He twirls in his chair to read the time, then twirls back facing me. He tidies his paperwork. He tucks away loose pens into side drawers. He flips open today's *Toronto Star*, flailing out the pages from the centrefold, burying his face in them. "I've got all day. I mean, *I don't*, but the phrase fits. Lemme know when you know."

Bzzz! *Bzzz*!

Feldbrook clears his throat, then peeks at me from behind the newspaper. I bet he's waiting for me to reach for my phone, like last session. But I won't. I want to, but I won't. Because what he just asked has me troubled — I've been running up and down all these gyms my entire life but have yet to ask myself…

Am I a winner?

Obviously he's not asking about the dusty trophies and medals in my closet, or whether I've made Ma, Pop, or Leena proud, or even whether I think I'm renowned as some, I dunno, *big shot* who's sought after as the guy everyone wants on their team because of what I bring to the table. No, that's not what he asked...

Am I ... a winner?

I draw in a breath, searching for an answer that I could live with, really. My eyes wander onto the patterns in the ceiling, the rich wood grain running smoothly along Feldbrook's bookshelves.

Then suddenly I'm caught by the headline on the *Star*'s front page, scrunched in Feldbrook's hands: *KING... SEARCH... SITED. What's it say*?

I tell him, "I don't know, Doc. But I wanna be a winner. A winner that aligns with whatever you're saying."

"Why?" He rests the newspaper on his desk, luring me into squinting at those upside-down words without even knowing. "Why with what *I'm* saying?"

"It makes sense to me. It gets me."

"But that's just it! You couldn't've had the same beliefs of winning or purpose or self-evolvement before stepping into my office today. So, you couldn't've believed in what I think a winner is," says Feldbrook, now cross-armed and leaning forward.

SHOCKING... SEARCH... REVISITED.

My heart sinks. *What's it say*! *Sit up, Feldbrook. Practice good posture. You're a doctor, you should know that*!

"You with me? What're you staring at?"

"Nothing, nothing."

"Are you a winner, Udoka?"

"Like I said, I wanna be a winner. 'What's real to me, what isn't,' you ask. I'm not sure. I don't know what's real anymore, with this hoops thing. But before I can become a winner, in whichever way I view 'winning,' I gotta filter out what matters from what doesn't, right?"

"Uh-huh ... right..."

"From what you're saying, if I could play for what really matters, *to me* — joy, growth, the thrill of competing, anything positive when I step on the court — then that's winning?"

He shrugs. "I don't know, is it?"

"I don't know!"

Feldbrook breaks out laughing. "Look, kid. If you're looking for a yes-or-no for what makes *you* flourish, then you'll leave here confused and unsatisfied. Because I don't have the answers, only the questions provoking you to find them."

"You got the time, at least?" He turns a shoulder to the clock again, as I hurriedly make out the words on that headline.

SHOCKING EVIDENCE: SEARCH FOR HOODED MAN REVISITED

I dig into my jeans for my phone then open Mo's message thread.

"Shoot! Time's up," Feldbrook says.

"Yeah, I gotta go!" I abruptly rise from my seat and snag the newspaper. "Hope you don't mind, Doc!"

CHAPTER XIII

SWING 'N A MISS

PAST

I returned to Toronto after spring finals, dragging home a heap of baggage. *Baggage*, not luggage — well, luggage too, but I'm talking about the heavy burdens of disappointment, of uncertainty, of failure, after a senior season filled with ups and downs.

I'd imagined it my last-chance, breakout, best year yet. The season where I'd turn heads and flood Instagram feeds with crowd-crazed highlights; where I'd build a list of scholarship offers to choose from; where I'd leave my nagging confidence issues in the past, *for good*.

Those unfulfilled visions came to mind when I plodded through the front door. "*Welcome hooome*!" Ma cheered. She was ecstatic to see me but clueless as to why her excitement wasn't reciprocated.

I unpacked my bags and found Coach Quinn's reports again. I pored over the words that jumped out from the page — *Soft ... Lacks confidence* — wishing I'd paid more attention to what those words truly meant when I had read them the first time.

Then I rediscovered that third-grade diary booklet; revisiting the ambitious mind of a child who had the world as his oyster, musing about the things he wrote, the desires he had. The mere thought of chasing this boy's hoop dream became overwhelming once the NCAA signing period had begun. With no Division 1 offers, my future seemed bleak.

Landing a full-ride D-1 scholarship was still possible the following year, though; had I stayed at Carinci Prep to "touch up on my grades." Believe me, that isn't at all taboo — hoopsters squeezing in an extra season of exposure hoping to make it into the NCAA, even when their marks were already tight, like mine were. Up here, that's called taking a "victory lap"; in the States they call it "reclassifying." It's the same deal how I see it, but it wasn't for me.

Because fortunately, there were already a handful of coaches from Canadian schools keeping tabs on me since my Oakwood days. Like Coach Maythorn, for example, to whom I paid a visit just weeks after returning home from Illinois. I didn't know much about him or his basketball program, but he seemed all right. He tossed me a grey sweatshirt that unfolded in my lap. It read *JOIN THE 'PACK* and had a sick shot of me getting up for a dunk in a Wolfpack uniform. It was a cool deal.

Maythorn was cool, too. He spoke to me as a person, not just as some ballplayer who could help him win some games. Yet even though he delivered a strong pitch, Maythorn didn't coach a Division 1 school — and that was all the reason why the 'Pack didn't appeal to me at first.

But see, I felt guilty staring at this modest pile of mail from schools that I at the time had little to no interest in entertaining. Before I left for Illinois, there was a stack of untouched envelopes sitting in my bedroom, simply because the thought of opening those envelopes, reading those letters, wrapping my head around playing on my native side of the border or at *any* non-D-1 school just wasn't part of my plan. I know — *ungrateful me*.

I used to check the mailbox and hope for something — *anything* — from some coach of whichever D-1 school, overly thrilled the few times I'd find a package worth feeling hopeful about, but often to no avail. I'd skim through a cookie-cutter blurb about "fine-tuning my SATs" or a vague invitation to that school's "Elite Camp," but never anything substantial, concrete. Never an inkling that an offer was on its way.

But after I had returned home, I eventually made a slit across every single one of those dust-collecting envelopes, having realized that I was fortunate to garner the interest of *any* school to begin with, and I was honoured to find that many of them still made a strong push for me. I probably wouldn't've heard the end of it if I didn't come to my senses, anyway. Throwing away good opportunities like that — I could just imagine Ma's response: "Tuition won't be coming outta *my* pocket then! Quite some nerve you got. Basketball's not everything! What, you're gonna get a degree in basketball, too?"

I mean, how would that've panned out? How could I have told Ma there'd been a handful of schools willing to fund my education, but they weren't the right ones — no matter how prestigious they were or how well-equipped I'd become to land that respectable "plan B" job she'd want me to have? But since they weren't one of the three-hundred-something programs competing for a ticket to the Big Dance — I was supposed to turn them down? Since they weren't one of the three-hundred-something programs with pro scouts flocking to sold-out arenas, searching for the next superstar — they weren't for me?

It was tough letting go of that lifelong dream; I was too hard-headed to let a "plan B" have me think twice about what I felt I was born to do. I didn't grow up wanting to be a doctor or lawyer or CEO or anything like that. When I was young, I used to have this flawed idea that the world's *whatever-ologists* and suit-and-tie execs weren't meant for people with my type of melanin, simply because the only rich and accomplished Black men I'd idolized and seen on TV, read about in the magazines, or listened to on the radio, could either leap forty inches off the ground or throw down with the mic. Ma couldn't blame me for wanting that for my life as well, for trying to measure up to that narrow metric of success — because back then, I thought *that* was all there was for me to become.

So when I stared at that dotted line and thought hard about inking the next four years of my life away to Coach Maythorn's university — though a fine institution, situated right by home — Ma couldn't blame me for having cold feet, either. But it was all right, because I had to find a way to keep the dream alive.

PRESENT

"And that brought you here?" asks Feldbrook.

"It did."

"And how did that go for you?"

I mumbled, "It brought me *here*, didn't it? To see you."

"So?"

"*So.* I'm a university-level athlete seeing a shrink for

my petty sports problems. Wasn't what I thought I'd sign up for when I was that eight-year-old kid."

"And what does that mean?"

"Means I had something planned for myself when I was young and hopeful. That *me* would've wanted to know if his wishes eventually came true. I owed it to myself to have had those dreams manifest. But I came up short."

"C'mon, it's not too late," Feldbrook tells me softly. "You have years ahead, remember? Wasn't that why you came to me in the first place — to play or not to play?"

"Regardless, Doc. Next season or no next season, the game's not the same anymore, man."

"Look, kid. You can still heal and change your outlook."

I stomp and exclaim, "No, it's over! I failed!"

Feldbrook snickers.

"Keep laughing, Doc!"

"Look at me." He settles into his chair, waiting for my frustration to simmer. "You did *not* fail."

"To you!"

He ponders for a second. "You know any baseball? I see you eyeballing my ring all the time, so I had to ask. Do you know a thing or two about it?"

I scowl at him, muttering, "Yeah, man. I catch the Jays once in a while. I know some. Hit a ball, run around a diamond. Whatever that has to do with anything."

"Okay. Take the best hitters in the Majors. What are they batting?"

"What?"

"In ten at-bats, how many are they hitting?"

"Beats me. Who cares?"

Feldbrook thumps his desk and bellows, "How many do they hit!"

"I dunno, five."

"*Three*! As talented as they are, they're hitting at maybe just above a three-hundred batting average."

I shrug. "So?"

"*So*, you're telling me that the best of the best, getting paid gazillions to hit a baseball about three times out of ten — all the while handling the pressure, the odds set against them — still have the confidence to strut to the plate—"

"But?"

"But you don't have it in you to believe in yourself when you're doing what you love? You don't have it in you to carry on after a few not-so-great seasons?"

"I hoop. I don't swing bats."

"Fair," he replies. "Fine. Riddle me this. Think about the superstars in the NBA right now — you name 'em. You think they shoot the lights out *every* game? You think they *never* get scored on? You think they survive entire seasons without throwing the ball away, not even *once*?"

I shake my head.

"No. Exactly. They make mistakes. So do their opponents. Every play!"

"Nah ... *every* play, Doc?"

"Oh, absolutely! My basket is your weak defense. Your steal and breakaway slam-jam comes from my sloppy ball control. Mistakes are what make the games interesting! The superstars always believe their next play will be game-changing, even when their last few weren't. They believe in their skills and shoot the same shot, regardless of whether they've scored ten in a row or missed their past twenty. Regardless of whether they've just hit an out-of-the-park homer or have swung at air for as long as they can remember. You gotta forget about what happened and focus on the next play, good or bad!"

"Guess this explains my frigid night from the field in the quarterfinals. Made my first shot with the clock winding down, then I went ice-cold. After halftime, I hardly even took a glimpse at the hoop."

"Shoot your shot, kid. Why stop trying?"

"Because ... I failed, man. I dunno."

He snickers again, saying, "There is no failure. We all mess up."

"No, you don't understand. It was this kind of thing all season. I failed Maythorn. My teammates. Myself. *All year*. A screw-up would get me benched, which would cause me to fret about that screw-up, leading to this weird, nervous feeling — hoping that I won't screw up the next time I'd get out there on the floor, 'cause in the back of my mind I could only imagine screwing up some way or another — *then* I'd screw up, then I'd fret some more, and—"

"All right, all right! I don't think you heard me the first time, kid! *There is no failure.*"

"Right."

"No, seriously!"

I asked Feldbrook what he was getting at, and here's how he broke it down...

FELDBROOK'S LESSON

Failure doesn't exist. We sometimes get too strung out on this idea of success versus failure. Success gets placed on this steep, gold-plated pedestal, while failure is viewed as something that should be avoided, punished, *feared.* When really, *failure* is subjective to one's own expectations — just like success, accomplishment, and self-worth are.

Sure, you can say, 'Failure *does* exist: you can't meet the passing grade for your exam — you *fail* the test; you clank a shot, badly or often — you're *failing* at scoring a basket.' Well, fair. In that sense, the distinction between 'failure' and 'success' is certainly existent. But it's that same idea that gets people fearing failure in the first place.

Your shortcomings are what lead you onto a distinct path.

Think of them as the necessary experiences that allow you to reroute, adapt, grow. It's getting that exam handed back to you, spotting your grade on the front page circled with thick red marker and realizing you didn't get the mark you wanted. It's that '*I know I'm better than this*' voice in your head, encouraging you to explore new strategies to learn and grasp the content, regardless of your grade.

It's the shots you miss that make the journey that much more meaningful. *Miss* that shot. Love the fact that you *missed* that shot. Embrace that experience more than if it weren't a misfire at your target. Because it'll all be worth it when you score.

Success can occur in a single moment; for example, you shoot your shot and watch the ball swish through the net. That thrill pumping through your veins should make you feel great, and that gratifying moment depends wholly on how long you choose to celebrate — which is your 'subjective' success. You can let your wrist hang for as long as you want after sinking that shot.

But in reality, it's all very brief, and that 'objective' success — that made shot — is over right after the ball returns to the floor: the scorer's table tallies a few points to your name, the opposing team retrieves the ball for their inbound, and you run back on defense to find your matchup. That's it — the 'success' of a made basket explained over just a few seconds.

'Failure,' though, is *a process.* It's not determined

by missing your first shot, or committing your tenth mistake, or when feeling like you haven't done anything right in a while. Failure only occurs when you decide it does and is, therefore, in no way an objective outcome. To fail means you've accepted defeat, you've surrendered to the obstacles laid out in front of you and think they're insurmountable.

Failure is a subjective process because *you* decide when to feel defeated. *You* decide when your obstacles cannot be surmounted, and when they're not worth another ounce of your effort. Until you decide to give up, failure isn't real.

When you take a shot, don't fear missing. Shoot! Shoot another time. And if again unsuccessful, shoot some more. But learn from your errors; don't pursue success with aimlessness. You wouldn't shoot the ball without aiming, would you? Shoot with correction. Shoot your shot after the hours, days, weeks, months of bettering your craft. Whether you decide to shoot after repeated misses is solely your choice.

Because, eventually, you *will* score again.

We've all heard it before — '*can't*' *should never be in your vocabulary*, *you can do anything you put your mind to,* and so on. Well, the terms '*can't*' and '*can*' are literally polar opposites. The transition from being unable to accomplish something, to being able to accomplish it, is not simple. It's a process.

'*I can't*' is negative, limiting. '*I can't*' says, 'I didn't accomplish my goal and I won't try again. It's over.' '*I can't*,' fails.

Tell yourself '*I haven't*' instead, as though to say, 'I haven't done it yet, but I'll try again, and eventually I'll do it.' If the goal remains unaccomplished, tell yourself the same thing. Again. And again. Then again, until you've earned the right to say, '*I can.*'

After a miss, it doesn't matter if you'll make the next one but if you're willing to *take* the next one. Because when you tell yourself that you *can't* score, only then may you *fail*. So, don't get discouraged, because those misses will provide a wealth of lessons that lead you on to a new journey toward the next made basket — on whichever type of hoop you're shooting.

CHAPTER XIV

OUTNUMBERED

McInnis is quiet and still. I plod through the corridor and up the stairs with heavy steps and heavy thoughts. Past the hallway of varsity locker rooms, I can feel the basketballs thudding to the floor. I press the wide-glassed doors ajar and see Louis and Conrad getting some shots up. Elvin is at the far end of the court, planting his stance for a free throw.

They dribble and jump and shoot, but they don't notice me. I see them grimacing with razor-sharp concentration. I see their passion. Their presence. Their impression that they enjoy being exactly where they are, doing exactly what they're doing. It's quite something.

The early offseason has given us plenty of gym time because we no longer need to share a tight schedule with other teams. Yet since it began a few weeks ago, I haven't joined a pickup run, let alone a game of H-O-R-S-E. This isn't my first time looking on from behind these tall glass panels, though.

The thought of Pop catches me here. I wonder if he knew what happened these past years, and what he'd think if I were to play out my eligibility. Or what he'd think if I wouldn't live out my Senior Day, down the road.

My guess is beyond me.

* * *

I'm hesitant to approach his office. Not Feldbrook's. Maythorn's. I gently knock on his door to find him caught by surprise.

"What's up, Duke?"

"Hey, Coach." I'm nervous and unsettled, and he can tell. I'm waiting for him to ask what brings me here. I had the entire conversation planned out in my head to make this as short and easy and to-the-point as it needs to be. So, he *needs* to ask what brings me here.

But he doesn't. Forget it. I'll just get it over with, blurt it out: "Basketball's not fun like it used to be, Coach. I don't feel like I ... like I—"

"It's okay, Duke. I know," says Maythorn. "You don't gotta explain yourself. It's no secret you're not enjoying this anymore, so I'm not surprised you're here. I'm *disappointed*, but I'm not surprised."

"I've ... y'know ... it's been..."

"A rough year for you. Yeah, I know." He nods consolingly, his arms crossed. "You've been iffy all season. Guess it took a toll on your morale. It's okay. I know. It's unfortunate 'cause, frankly, I like you. As a teammate to the guys, as a person. You managed to bring something to the table in spite of whatever's been going on in your head. The team's grown fond of you, Duke. It's disappointing how your first year went, but I want what's best for you. And if being away from the team and the game is what you need, then you bet I'll support your decision."

"C-Coach..." I stutter, overwhelmed as I realize that this is it — the end of what has been a lifelong journey. I see flashes of the ball bouncing when I was young and spirited. I reminisce about the cheerful times and the difficult times, too, with Pop and the friends I've made along the way: the Keeles, the Rons, the Elvins. I relive the vision of having a spotlight follow me in a dark, filled arena as I skip onto the floor, hearing my name announced before tip-off. I come to terms knowing that I hadn't ever lived out this dream in the NCAA and I won't at the pro level, but I've at least been privileged to experience it here, at this tip-top school.

If only I had some more fight in me, was a little more enduring, more steadfast — maybe basketball would've panned out differently. But for the *better*? It scares me wondering if the fighting, enduring 'me' would've put himself through prolonged damages just to see basketball through to the end. It scares me wondering if people would've seen him as admirable — valiant, even — despite him possibly dying inside and beneath that jersey for years to come…

These thoughts consume me as I look over at Maythorn and say, "Thank you. It's … it's been a story, Coach."

* * *

Feldbrook flips open his notepad for a blank page.

"I don't think we've delved into your timeline since enrolling here," he says, unaware that I just quit the team. "So, Oakwood, then you finished your final years of high school in the States, Carinci Prep. You committed here after that. Then what? You earned a starting spot to begin the season, if I'm not mistaken."

"I did."

"And so?"

"I lost it."

"And how did that make you feel?"

"Angry. I was mad."

"Well, that's not a bad thing, right! You were upset — you lost an opportunity that meant something to you. It shows you still care, which is positive, right?"

"I wasn't angry for losing the starting spot," I confess. "I was angry, distraught, confused as to why I *wasn't* angry about losing it. I was conflicted because losing that opportunity — an opportunity I had earned by working my ass off my whole life, an opportunity I had always cared about and strived for at this level — wasn't a concern to me anymore. I guess the fire within me had been put out for good, long before I realized there was no use in trying to rekindle it."

"I take it you didn't have a good year."

"Damn sure didn't," I mumble. "I never reached a clear mind."

"Meaning something was disrupting it."

"Well, mentally, I was always worrying about things that shouldn't've mattered. *What will the commentators say on the livestream if I make my first shot? How will people treat me on campus if I'm named Player of the Week?* Or thoughts like, *Can I survive this quarter without throwing the ball away? How will I look if I clank both of these free throws? How will Maythorn react? What will people in the crowd have to say about that? If I screw up, what are people gonna think of me? What will my teammates think?*"

Feldbrook drops his pen and waits for silence. "It's a five-on-five sport," he says. "One team against the other in healthy competition. Ten humans — *humans* — that breathe the same air and bleed the same blood. On the court, there's nothing to worry about, kid."

I clear my throat. "One-on-three, the way I see it."

"Pardon?"

"The five guys on the other team, yeah, I got that. I'll count 'em as one opponent. But then you got Maythorn, he's the second. Feels like he's just expecting me to screw up so he can yank me off the court and onto the bench, even when that's probably not the case."

"Right. It's *not*. If he calls upon you to enter the game, it's because he believes you'll do good things, make big plays. Believe me, you wouldn't've had any business on that court if he felt you weren't cut out for it."

"I'm not done!" I snap. "There's me, myself. I'm opponent number three. I got this stupid voice in my head telling me I'll lose my dribble, or ruin a play, or get crossed up by some mediocre kid that deep down I know I can check, even on my worst day. It's like I'm held back by my self-doubt. Forget five-on-five, man. This game's about one-on-one battles. I mean, yeah, obviously you got your team and they got theirs. Ten guys on the floor. I get all that. But,"— I gather a breath, catching a glimpse of Feldbrook's confusion, well aware that I'm rambling — "it's really you against the man in front of you. Mano a mano, and the better man wins. And I feel like that's the case for everybody, but—"

"But you? Feels like you're battling two other opponents?" Feldbrook replies, seeking some sort of clarification.

He's right. Basketball somehow became one-on-three to me, and despite what went down between Maythorn and I just a moment ago, I'm all ears for whatever Feldbrook's about to tell me. It's ought to be something insightful...

FELDBROOK'S LESSON

Cancel out the noise. Listening to what people say about us is normal. Critiques keep us in check, while flattery feeds our self-esteem. But we shouldn't dwell on the criticisms or latch on to the compliments we receive.

Negative opinions — whether hurtful or even meant as constructive feedback — can sometimes bring down your spirit. These comments could corrode your ego, destroy your sense of *self*, and eat away at your confidence.

When peoples' remarks bring down your confidence, you may start second-guessing yourself and believing in the negativity — even though you *know* what you're capable of.

No one understands the challenges you've undergone or the obstacles you've surpassed as thoroughly as you do. You've experienced your journey first-hand; you know your strengths and flaws better than anyone else — which means *you* have the clearest signal of that voice in your head, articulating the vision of who *you* want to become.

So, cancel out the negative noise.

What about the praise, the compliments, the 'tooting of one's horn?' Sure, these boost our morale when we're down and stroke our egos, make us feel good. But that's also filling your mind with what *other people* think of you, what other people want you to accomplish. This can distort your self-concept. It can distract you from finding your true purpose, from fulfilling your goal of becoming the best possible *you*.

Basking in praise can open the door to validation seeking as well, which can render you too attentive to the noisy voices of people and their expectations of you.

Why cancel out *these* noises? Well, when you can't meet peoples' expectations or aren't receiving the recognition you feel you deserve, your self-worth could become dictated by outside opinions. And even if you *can* meet or exceed peoples' expectations, you might never be enough for them, finding yourself reaching for their validation that'll always be an inch away, no matter how high you climb. Both scenarios can eat at your confidence, and those feelings of self-acceptance, self-worth — you may not attain them if you seek them from other people.

You've likely stumbled upon this phrase at some point: *If you think you can or if you think you can't — chances are, you're right.* Let that be *your* decision, not someone else's. Cancelling out the noise means listening to but not internalizing what others say about you. You are your own person; you can think for yourself. What you think you can or can't do, what is *real* to you, what is true to who *you* are — should not be tampered with by external sources. Only *you* should determine your limits. You, and only you, should define your purpose.

Protect your *self*. Your *self* is your home. Don't let anyone else in. The visitors can give a quick word at the doorstep, but don't undo the locks and open the door. Keep them out. Don't let them occupy the clear space that houses your thoughts; don't let them muffle the internal voice of your goals, visions, and aspirations. Because their voices are noisy. Cancel out the noise.

* * *

"So in the end, it doesn't matter, huh?"

"Does *what* not matter?" Feldbrook asks.

"What other people think."

"As it concerns your life and how you choose to live it, no."

My head sinks to my knees. I find myself looking vacantly at the floor.

"What's bothering you?" he asks. "Something's up."

"This's our last session, right?"

"Yep, it is. You can schedule more with the registrars if you'd like. But you've made progress, kid."

Silence seeps into the room. Still, I am downcast, as though everything weighing on my mind is doing so quite literally.

"So what if I choose to forego next season? I've been thinking about some things."

"Things like what?"

"Like, what am I gonna do without ball? I'm straight with my grades and all — I mean, I guess I listened when my mum drilled that 'plan B' stuff into my head — but this is what I've done, this is who I've been all my life. What, I'm supposed to just *quit*? What'll the guys in the locker room think? What about Pop, what'll he say? How'll I break it to him?"

"What will *you* have to say, Udoka?"

"But I'm asking about them."

"And I'm asking about *you*."

"Well, I'm ... I think I'm ready ... to hang 'em up. Hang up the kicks."

"Okay. Understood. Coach's office is down the hall, did you know?"

"Oh. Wasn't aware." I lied.

"These emotions — you're not saying much, but I can tell there's lots you have to spill. You're about to make a pivotal decision right now, letting go of something so essential to you. Somewhere deep down are emotions that are raw and real, and finally coming together. I won't keep you, Udoka."

"All right." I rise from my chair, hesitantly.

"Before you go," Feldbrook adds, "just remember what brought you here to begin with. Remember that eight-year-old boy in your heart whose vision was pure and without worry or fear. Remember he never anticipated having any doubts that would interfere with reaching his destiny. Remember he envisioned himself looking back on his story, years later, reflecting on his journey and the passion he put into it — without any concern for external rewards, or what others thought about him or what made his life meaningful. Remember that hopeful, eight-year-old boy. He wished for a world in which nothing else but this one, true passion — this one thing that gave him a heartbeat, a breath, a twinkle in his eyes — mattered."

"Okay … okay, Doc. I'll remember."

"He never wanted you here. By *here*, I mean literally — you talking to an old fogey like me about your feelings. You wouldn't be sitting across from me if you hadn't lost sight of what that little boy was all about. Will you quit, will you play — I don't know. I'm not here to help you decide. But regardless, just remember that he still exists, that little boy. Search, and you'll find him. You'll find clarity."

"All right."

"All right."

"Doctor Feldbrook. Thank you."

He bows his head. "Take care, Udoka."

I take a long look at him before shutting his door.

Down the hallway, there's a slit of light glimmering on the floor in front of Maythorn's office. I'm toying with the idea of rescinding my farewell — an afterthought of all the sentiments I've just taken in.

I stare down the hallway and then at that glowing blade of light in the tiles for as long as time can elude me.

My stomach churns. I turn around and walk away.

CHAPTER XV

HERE, YOU ARE

Staring in the mirror is afflicting. I'm tormented into accepting the ugly insecurities, the imposter on the other side. I see a coward. A spineless, unenduring coward. A quitter! *A quitter*? *Me, a damn quitter*? I don't recognize him, this '*me.*'

Basketball was all I had known and everything I had become. This love once seemed everlasting, constant. But now it's nothing. She began to lose me, just as I began losing myself. My body and soul, in sync no longer; I'm a stranger to my own being.

I'm caught on that day at Woolner Park when Pop introduced Her into my life. He told me to honour Her, cherish Her — intensely, unconditionally, every single day. And I did that, for as long as I could. She was everything I ever needed, long before I had even known.

She taught me how to dream, how to obsess, how to devote my life to something meaningful, something real. She showed me bliss and boundless elation, but also pain and harrowing sorrows. She shared a wealth of lessons, teaching me how to laugh and how to cry; most of all, though, She taught me how to feel.

But *feel*? I can't do that anymore.

My unconditional love for Her has run dry. I mourn Her absence, though we'll soon grow apart. The hoop posters pinned across the four walls in my room feel like they never belonged to begin with. Sneakers that I'd played in are probably buried under loose clothes and boxes in my closet. My trophy collection has embraced a coat of dust that dims its shine. My feet no longer jitter, nor do my palms moisten to a warm clamminess for that itch to lace up and play.

Time will proceed without Her, my first love. She's not even a thought in my mind. I renounce *Yoosie*, that high-spirited kid with a world of potential and a promising hoop dream. I am Udoka now. Nothing more.

* * *

It's a chilly morning. Thick flurries sprinkle the Jane Street sidewalk as I drag my heavy, Timberland-shod feet toward Bloor. From the corner of my eye, I spot someone clomping back and forth along the Jane Station terminal, keeping warm, I suppose. By some fluke, that someone spots me too. He's now stopped in his tracks, clogging traffic for the commuters herding into the idling buses.

Could it be … him? He waves from afar, but I don't react, hoping he assumes I didn't notice him behind the heavy snowfall.

Regardless, he approaches.

"It's me, Udoka!" he calls. "Wait! Hol' up!" I plod through slush, heading back north on Jane and trying to lose him, but he hollers louder, and I can sense him nearing. "It's me! Wait a sec!" I pick up my pace, hurried by the wind whipping my cheeks. "Aight! Cool! I put a ball in your hands! Just 'member that!"

Damn. He's right … I don't know if giving him the cold shoulder'll sit well with me later on. Because, after all, here he is, pleading for my time during an awful snowstorm. Eventually, I come to my senses. I gotta turn back.

"What."

"Whatcha been up to?" he asks, removing his hood and scarf despite the weather, revealing a coarse beard that makes him totally unrecognizable from when I'd last seen him. He's in cargo pants and a fleece hoodie beneath a quilted flannel jacket, fraying along the collar. His shoes are soiled at the toes, and his hands are bare but sheltered under his jacket's cuffs. He shudders, awaiting a response. Who knows — a quick "hi and bye" could mean a lot to him.

"Nothing. I've been good," I tell him, grimacing in the cold. "School and all. You?"

"I'm hangin' in there." He looks me in the eye, the wind punishing his face. "You go get your degree, Udoka. No one could take your education from you." *Yeah, whatever.* "How's Leena these days? You got a missus yet? How's she?"

"They're good, Pop."

"And basketball, you still doin' your thing?" I'm stalling for a response, pondering the quickest excuse. But he cuts in anyway: "You gonna play at that Hoops 'n Hearts tourney, right?"

"The *what*?" I respond, seeming perplexed, I hope. The "what-are-you-talking-about" front isn't my strong suit.

The Hoops 'n Hearts Classic is an annual charity tournament for heart disease research, with proceeds donated to a few hospitals downtown, so it's a cool deal. The top players from all corners of the city suit up and play for nothing more than the bragging rights of being crowned Toronto's best — from the tykes to the men's and women's divisions.

"C'mon, man! Check out this flyer." Pop reaches into his pocket and pulls out a print ad. Along the border it reads *HEALTHY HOOPS FOR HEALTHY HEARTS,* with a silhouette dribbling a basketball in a plain jersey. Pop then reaches for my hand, shivering, forcing the flyer on me. "They were handing these out at work. Some sponsorship thing going on," he explains. "Anyway, you gonna play or what?"

"Where … where've you been … all this time?"

"I can't get into all that. Just promise you'll be there. Put on a show for me, man!"

The irony of Pop using that word around me, especially after what I've just asked him! Those camps and tournaments in the States come to mind — the last time he's "been there" for *me*. Aside from those trips, even, it's been a minute since he's truly been around.

"Yeah," I respond anyway. "Promise."

I watch him take a good look at me, as though he's troubled by accepting that this moment is limited, that this moment has no sympathy for whatever he wants to tell me that could make up for lost time. Because really, this was meant to be a *brief* exchange, if anything, so as he's gazing at the few years of growth he'd missed out on witnessing, I bet he's contemplating what he could say to make this moment memorable, long-lasting, heartfelt. "It's … it's good seeing you," he says instead, pointing to the flyer as we go our separate ways.

* * *

It isn't until I'm underground, waiting for the next train heading eastbound, where I process what just happened: Pop's persistence, his audacity squeezing a promise out of me, the randomness of it all, the *nerve of him.* Little does he know I'm scrunching his stupid flyer into a tight paper ball, soon to be tossed away. I mean, why should I play? To please *him*?

Along the narrow platform where the commuters gather, I spot a trash bin; and from a couple steps away, I take a shot at it. The paper ball grazes the bin and lands on the cold, wet ground.

Ironic, huh? Yeah, whatever.

* * *

Keele and I stumbled into each other during a layover along Line 2. He'd been telling me how he finally earned a starting spot on his college team after bouncing around from school to school as a redshirt, then as a walk-on, and now as his squad's main PG. It's been a while since we last spoke, but looking at him I still see the same grit and resilience from high school that led him to his little glories. I'm glad he finally got his shot. There's no mistaking why a school finally gave him one — he just never gave up.

I'm reluctant to tell him I quit basketball after he asked how it's been going for me. And while he nods as though he understands my decision, I can sense he's disappointed; I can sense how deeply he cannot relate with the reasons I'm giving him; he probably wants to blurt out how big a mistake I made. Instead, he's giving me the benefit of the doubt, since I'm doing "whatever makes me happy," he says. *Yeah, whatever.* I bet he senses this divide between us too, the way he's so eager to veer the conversation toward how well he's been playing. For what it's worth, I'm pleased to listen.

"Eight, five, and two."

"Two what? Rebounds or assists?" I ask.

"Nah, *steals*, bro! Eight points, about five dimes, and two picked pockets a game."

"So how many rebounds you averaging?"

"About the same as Coach," he scoffs, as we share a laugh. "You see my size, man. I don't battle for no damn boards!"

"Yeah, just keep that a secret from him."

"Coach reads the stats too! He knows I'm above all that boxing-out shit. But if he needs me to zip down the court for a quick bucket, I'm his guy!" I cackle once again. "I got a scrimmage 'gainst some college from out West, on Friday. They're comin' all that way just to get blown out! Imma give 'em twenty, maybe twenty-five. You gotta come watch me hoop, Yoosie." Keele's confidence is refreshing. He's got a zeal, a passion that would inspire any hoopster, but for my jaded self, it's nostalgic.

"I'll let you know."

"You'll *lemme know*? It'll be official! Scoreboards, refs, all the—"

"Eh, that's all solid. I'll let you know, though."

"Well, whatcha got going on this Friday?" Keele asks. "Wait..." He freezes. "Don't tell me you're..." I begin nodding. "You can't be." Again, I dip my head. "Studying? Fam ... on a *Friday night*?"

"On a Friday night."

Keele looks stunned. "That's what it's like, really?"

"What *what's* like?"

"The whole school-and-no-ball thing. That's nuts!"

Yeah, you're telling me.

"Where're you headed, anyway?" I ask him.

"The gym, bro!"

"No class?"

"I mean, yeah, kinda. *Sorta*," he admits, gripping the nearest handrail while the train rocks from side to side, a leather Spalding cradled in his other hand. "I got class: Music and Humanities. This exam review thing."

I smirk at Keele, shaking my head.

"Damn, sorry, youngin'! Didn't know you cared so much! Besides, you know how many dudes take bullshit majors just so they can hoop? This one guy on my team's in Floral ... Floral Sustainability, or he was telling me it's called Floral Management or something. Some mess like that."

I ask him, "What's he gonna do with that when he's done playing?"

"Clean gooey popcorn off the floor at the theatre, maybe."

Keele starts chuckling, and I smirk too. "Eh, 'whatever makes him happy,' like you told me."

He replies, "Or his *wifey* happy, at least. Floral Management — that's roses galore for her on Valentine's Day!" The two of us burst into laughter, bringing life to this vacant space of maroon, velvet seats, and steel bars.

Though after the giggles settle, he gets quiet; he knows what I'm about to ask.

"What about you, Keele?" He's downcast, gazing down the aisle. "What's *your* plan when ball's done?"

He draws in a breath, now looking out the window for the winter scenery. "It won't be. After this, I'm going straight to the League. And if not, I'll do the overseas thing first, then make my way into the League after that."

"You got something lined up?"

"Nah." He hangs his head. "Not yet. It'll come, though." Keele probably knows he's being stared at — the way he could just spill his "foolproof" pipe dream as if it's often you'll find a Canadian sub-six-footer ink a deal to the NBA just like that. Especially from here and *not* the NCAA — with the growing-yet-still-minimal college-level exposure we have up North, coupled with his not-so-special stats — I bet he knows I'm musing. He's just waiting for me to say something.

"Yeah, dope," I say.

"Look, I already know what you're gonna say, man. You're gonna tell me, 'There's gotta be a plan B,' like your mom used to shout. And the truth is..." He stops to face me. "I'm scared, 'cause I don't got one. This is all I know."

"What do you mean, Keele?"

"I mean ... they give us a ball and a hoop to play on from young and throw us in all these camps and tryouts. Telling us we could do it, we could make it, if we 'work hard or put our minds to it.' Having us buy into that idea, like there's a solid chance for everybody."

"I hear that. Hundred percent."

"The coaches I had when I was little — yeah, they preached how 'school comes first' and all that, but only 'cause you can't get no scholly with shit grades! They didn't tell me what that really meant, 'cause when ball's all said and done, what else do I got going for me? I mean, it doesn't even gotta be a *school thing* — just anything to keep you sane and make you some steady cash if ball can't.... *When* ball can't." Keele sighs, adding, "But what else do I got? They teach you how to dribble and shoot. They boost you up so you can believe you'll make it. But back then, you're too young to be disappointed. So, they couldn't tell you that the chance was already slim, or that only a handful from the bunch would climb to the other side of the fence — if those dudes were *lucky*! So, you get caught up in that dream and you run with it, and say, 'Screw everything else!' until down the road you realize you got no other outlets clicking for you like you thought they would. But then it's like, 'How could I blame Coach for *encouraging* me when I was younger? Was he *not* 'posed to root me on like that?' Especially when I'm seeing some of the guys we grew up playing against finally getting their shot..."

I can only nod to let Keele know that I'm with him. Because quite frankly, he has no clue that I feel nearly the same way — I just chose to accept my reality sooner.

"Yoosie. School's out for me in a couple months. I'm *graduating* a couple months after that. Then it's off to the 'real world,' where I gotta send out résumés for some job or whatever. Screw all that, man! *This* is my real world!" — he taps the basketball clutched to his waist — "This right here's the only job I'll apply for. I'm in too deep to change my whole game. It's ball or nothing. I got no plan B! Feel me?"

"Yeah, no doubt. That's all cool," I tell him, feeling it's the only thing a good friend *could* say.

"But my bad, homie. Didn't mean to get all emotional on you."

He reaches over with a loosely closed fist, as I do the same to have our fists tap together. "It's all good, Keele."

"Yo, so you can't watch me play Friday night — cool. At least join my squad for Hoops 'n Hearts come springtime. You said you were on board last year, but you bailed." *What, first Pop, now Keele, too*?

I shrug. "Why?"

"You don't wanna play?"

"What for? What's the point?"

"Whaddya mean?" asks Keele.

"What am I gonna do, throw down a few dunks and carry on like a little fun-and-games tourney will make me feel good? Makc up for the all the bad games I had? Hit a couple shots like I was doing that in college this whole time, when really I wasn't?"

"Nah, chill out, freshman," says Keele. "That's in the past. Just play!"

The train halts at Spadina Station, and the doors slide open.

"I'll let you know, man," I tell him. "This is me, though — gotta hop on the next train heading south." I harness the straps of my backpack. Keele nods at me as I step onto the exit platform and into a new day.

But something's telling me to turn back…

I think of Feldbrook and what he'd say right now, and how those sessions I spent searching for some kind of 'moral purpose' could all be put to use this one last time.

So I do turn back, before the doors slide shut. I jam my arm through them and pry them open. "Yo, Keele!" He turns his head to my voice. "I'm in! Save me a spot!"

CHAPTER XVI

[UN]FAMILIAR GROUNDS

I spot dozens of familiar people. The players on the court. The spectators in the crowd. I'm caught thinking about when or where I've last seen them.

I see old teammates from my tyke days whose limbs were once weak and scrawny beneath baggy uniforms but are now built and styled with all kinds of ink; opponents from this past season, for whom I've developed respect, as I've caught a glimpse of what it takes to play college-level ball and how it shouldn't at all be taken lightly.

My eyes wander across the several hardwood courts in this broad, dome-shaped facility, gazing at various faces, both old and new — people with their own stories, just like mine. It's chilling how deeply embedded basketball has become in Toronto, how a leather ball can gather all the boroughs under a single roof. There's this electric feeling in here; it has me anxious for what's to come this weekend.

I'm nervous, but excited. Feldbrook's voice echoes in my head: *Be confident … Embrace the failures … Enjoy the process … Try again.* These seem like simple cues, but not having even dribbled a ball since the season ended should bring on some jitters. Regardless, my goal is simple: play well this one last time with Pop in the crowd and have fun doing it. I figure the rest of my petty worries will dissolve if I can follow through with this one task.

My team's stacked with college guys who're playing at schools on both sides of the border. Many are having storied careers, some will surpass the thousand-point milestone, and a few even have a chance to play overseas. We're all cool with one another, some more than others, so there's already a chemistry heading into the tournament.

* * *

Our first game is underway; fifteen minutes 'til tip-off. I gallop along the sideline to the beat of the warm-up tunes. The heavy bass thumps through the speakers and gets my blood pumping.

Into the layup lines we split. Guys are giving high-fives. Cracking jokes. Sharing memories from their playing careers. Meanwhile, I'm doing whatever I can to reach some calm. Everyone seems so cool and collected; then there's me and my frantic self.

I need to relax.

Close your eyes. Breathe. I've done this before. I've been here before.

I toss the ball high right when I get it, letting it bounce just before the painted area so I can meet it at the rim. When it does, I corral it with both hands and swing my arms behind my body. Above the rim, I throw down a ferocious slam. *Boom*!

"You still got it like that, eh, Yoosie?" a surprised Keele shouts, slapping me five.

I shrug nonchalantly. "We'll find out."

Jogging into the rebound line, I watch my teammates swish past one another like traffic on a two-way street. They're bobbing their heads to the pregame music, eager to approach the hoop, one-by-one.

Pop used to tell me the way in which a player carries himself in layup lines could tell you a lot about his game, his journey, his identity. And more often than not, Pop's predictions were valid, like he was some sort of — I dunno — tarot card reader of amateur hoops or something. But instead of cards, it was how someone would dribble, or run, or do something particular when performing a chest pass, for example, that would lead Pop to believe that when the clock starts, that player will play soft, or arrogant, or lazy, or be the game's leading scorer, or what have you.

Just thinking of him sitting somewhere in these stands puts me on edge. What type of player would he label *me* as, had I been unknown to him? What would he think of the guys on my squad, even? If I could invade Pop's mind and guess what to expect from my teammates, I think their profiles would sound a little something like this:

First up — Alex Gustaliano, best known around town as *Goose*. He'll be our man in the middle protecting the basket. Goose stands six-foot-ten and was given the moniker due to this abnormally long, bendy structure that connects his head to the rest of his body. Some might call it a neck, but I have a neck, and mine isn't nearly like that! Goose is also sneakily athletic. He doesn't look the type to have a thirty-five-inch vertical, at a weight of what I'd guess is two hundred and fifty pounds — because when you watch him in action, he tends to keep his feet glued to the floor, but he can get airborne and reach heights that other players can't.

Goose looks heavily focused. He flips the ball to himself with his back facing the basket and pivots to the baseline, then he turns his shoulder toward the front of the net. He flicks the ball for a hook shot that rattles around the rim before sinking through the mesh.

There's Scotty Jeffreisen — *Scoot*, we call him — likely to start as our stretch-forward. He stands maybe six-foot-seven and is a bit stocky but can scamper down the floor like a gazelle. Scoot had an historic year at a D-2 program in the Midwest: he broke his school's record for the most threes made in a season and earned All-Conference honours despite partially tearing his rotator cuff during conference play. His hair is perfectly parted to the side with a modest amount of gel holding it in place. Scoot carries a strictly-business demeanour that mirrors his easy, conservative playing style: he sticks to his strengths and isn't enticed by the allure of adopting a new dimension to his game.

Scoot waits his turn, flailing his arms in circles to mobilize his ailing shoulder. He catches the ball behind the arc and shoots it without even taking a dribble. So, like his sharpshooting résumé in college, there's no surprise when he sinks his first warm-up shot; the ball snaps the core of the mesh.

Behind Scoot trails Amarr Trite, or *Marr* for short. Marr wears a tall, curly afro with a low fade tapered by the ears, and a crisp shape-up with a fine slit by the side of his forehead. His shooting sleeve, calf-length compression tights, and low-cut sneakers resemble colours from a pack of assorted highlighters, with flashes of neon green, pink, and turquoise, respectively.

Marr was heavily recruited out of high school and earned multiple scholarship offers by the end of his senior year. But as a freshman this past season at a low-major D-1 school, he was blindsided by a culture shock that many rookies, like myself, encounter and aren't yet mature or disciplined enough to handle: honouring a curfew; maintaining an adequate GPA; attending team sessions that hadn't existed or definitely weren't mandatory in the seasons prior, such as shootarounds, film studies, and morning lifts; the distractions (i.e., parties, binge drinking, and flocks of girls wanting every chunk of his little free time — all of which hindered his capacity to do the above); the reduced minutes; the vanished *I'm-the-man* mentality; and the pressure of chipping away at his own game to match the rigid mold of his coach's simple-yet-steep expectations — these were all challenges he'd never been exposed to in high school.

So when I see Marr next in line, wrapping the ball behind his back a few times before crossing over for a finessed up-and-under finish on the other side of the board, I imagine a story of a player deprived of his own joy for the game; someone humbled by a rude awakening of what the "real" game is like where it "really" matters; someone who relishes any opportunity — like a charity tournament — to flap his wings the moment his cage opens.

Pop once said that the way you choose to warm up — whether you get up for monstrous dunks, get off a couple catch-and-shoot threes, or pound in your seven-dribble combo to get loose — has a way of introducing who you are as a player. It paints an image of your game that is yet to be showcased. But from what I've experienced, the pages in your story can vastly differ from the cover. You could put on this cool and cocky front during the warm-up but then play tentatively, iffy, scared. You can pull off all sorts of dunks during the layup lines, then become afraid to leave the floor when the game is on.

And that's my problem: at around the time I called it quits, I couldn't seem to find my identity on the court anymore, or the story my game wanted to tell. And I figure it's too late to reinvent who I am beneath this tight, reversible jersey.

Feldbrook's voice whispers in my head once more: *Pay no mind to others' judgments of the real you. Their opinions of your journey are null and void.*

* * *

Game one was forgettable.

This weird, startling feeling pulsed through me the moment I first touched the ball in the opening minutes; I felt like I was playing Hot Potato, the way I got rid of it so quickly. Everything Feldbrook had told me seemed to have gone right out the window, because I couldn't manage — not even once — to let myself be in the moment and enjoy the game, without a care for whether I'd take a shot to swish through the net or graze nothing at all. It was as though I was stuck in this charity event, watching my history sadly repeat itself.

Because it did.

For game two also. Game three as well.

Yet without any impact from me whatsoever, we've tallied two wins and a loss thus far and have advanced past round-robin play.

* * *

SATURDAY

Maureen McBendell *9:02AM*
Goooood luck!

Maureen McBendell *9:03AM*
Tell me how ur 1st game goes ok?

Maureen McBendell *12:12PM*
So???

Maureen McBendell *12:51PM*
When's the next one?

Maureen McBendell *12:57PM*
Missed call

Maureen McBendell *3:38PM*
Not cool. I get that u wanna focus but u can't shut me out!!!

Maureen McBendell *5:57PM*
Hellooo...How's it going? U kickin' butt?

Ah, crap. What should I say? "Sorry, love. Not really. I'm…" she'll just worry some more. Delete. "Sorry, Mo…" "Love" is fine. Go with "love."

All right, not bad.

I find myself hunched over on the bleachers after our third game, overwhelmed by disappointment. Whistles are blowing like the sound of crickets on a summer evening. Ten bodies dash back and forth; I feel rushes of air breezing by as they pursue the ball, and I wonder if any of them feel the way I did out there. I wonder if any of them are afflicted with their own anxieties, if any of them had let their guard down and spoken to someone for help, like I did — and for no good use, even. Because I imagine I can't be the only one, whatever consolation that'll provide. It can't only be me wondering if overcoming these troubling doubts is an impossibility that can't be fixed...

It's not only me; it can't be.

"Yo! Yoosie!" I turn to find Keele approaching along the narrow sideline. "What you still doin' here? You not hungry? Go get some grub before the semis tonight!"

"I'm straight."

"Scoot over real quick." Keele parks himself beside me, the same Spalding from that subway ride bouncing through his legs. "Lemme chop it up with you for a minute," he says.

"What's up?"

"You know how many dudes you're better than in here?"

"Really?"

Keele scrunches his face. "Never mind," he says, gathering his ball and rising from the bleachers. "If you don't believe that — that's cool. Imma go get some food."

"Eh, wait up!" I rip the ball from under his arm. "What were you saying!"

"I was saying you can play, bro," he replies, sitting back down. "Ever since those days at Woolner Park, I knew you had game. You're better than so many guys in here right now. F'real! But 'cause you doubt yourself, 'cause you got no confidence, you ... you got..."

"Nothing." I run my hands down my buzz-cut scalp, drooping forward.

Keele shakes his head. "Eh, look at it this way … at your best, you can shoot better, run faster, jump higher, guard probably anyone in this gym. If only—"

"What about you?" I blurt out. "Can I guard you? Am I better than you?"

"Hell nah!" he exclaims. "Nobody's checkin' me! Nobody's better than me! Not you, not a single chump in here!"

"Yeah, right."

Keele glares at me and goes, "No shit! That's what I believe! Imagine if you felt the same about yourself, Yoos. Imagine where you'd be if you got rid of that doubt, man. There's no place for it. 'Cause if we're one-on-one — you 'gainst me — you best believe I got no sympathy for you. Playing *scared* with all that weak stuff. You're just my prey at that point!"

"Yeah … that's facts."

"Yeah, fam," he goes. "Y'know, I've been thinking 'bout the other day — when we were on the train. The whole 'plan B' thing. Look at all these dudes in here…" Keele runs his pointed finger from one end of the gym to the other, and my eyes follow. "Like I said, some of these guys don't got no other option but ball. Some of them can't afford to play all scary. You got no time to second-guess yourself, no time for doubt. 'Cause the moment you do, *bam*! There goes your shot. *Bye-bye*! And you might not get another one. Feel me?"

"Yeah, Keele."

"Some of us only got one chance. And that one chance is ball. Think you'd be getting that uppity education if it weren't for this thing right here?" he asks, snagging his ball from me and cupping it in his palm. "I mean, for you, actually — yeah, probably. 'Cause you're one smart-ass dude. But ball helped pay for what you're learning, at least a lil' bit. Am I wrong?"

"No. You're not."

"Aight then!" Keele pops the Spalding back over to me then nudges my shoulder. "Whatever you do, man — I'm talkin' life, not only this just-for-fun tourney — be tough up here," he says, tapping both sides of his head. "Believe in yourself, Yoosie. No one's gonna believe in you if you don't."

I extend my arm out with an open palm, and Keele does the same as our hands slap and fold into each other. "Thanks," I tell him, wrapping my arm around his back. "I needed that." And as we get up to leave the gym, I can't help but imagine how much better I'll be the next time I enter these doors again. Whatever it takes, I *will* get my head straight for tonight's semis.

I need to.

CHAPTER XVII

WON'T SHOOT, CAN'T SCORE

The scoreboard reads 53–46. The clock's stopped at 4.2 seconds left in the third quarter of a lifeless semifinal, plagued by back-and-forth turnovers and questionable fouls called against both teams. My feet plant along the foul line as I peer into the dying crowd; it's nothing like it was at tip-off. I survey the bleachers for Pop as the ref with the shiny, black Reeboks tosses me the ball to shoot a pair.

My routine has always been the same: I'd take three calm dribbles and a deep breath. Then, I'd close my eyes and gather my concentration, reminiscing about the tranquil times of ten, nearly fifteen years ago at Woolner Park, with its faded foul stripes and round backboards. I'd envision Pop nearby, replacing this lousy ref, giving me pointers. "Set your feet straight," or, "Put some arc on it," he'd say.

I'm standing on this shiny floor fifteen feet from the hoop, having finally found Pop sitting alone in the highest row by the far baseline. His arms are stiffly crossed as he stares in my direction. Not a wave or a crack of a smile. Just a stare, bland and cold.

"Don't think. Just shoot it," says Marr from behind me. He probably thinks I'm hesitant to take the foul shot due to a confidence issue — which ultimately is true, but not at this very moment.

My first attempt rattles in after the ball bounces off the side of the rim then rolls around it. The horn sounds as Keele checks out of the game to avoid picking up a petty foul on the quarter's final play. One more and he's out, so playing it safe is his best bet. Replacing Keele comes Goose, who trots onto the court alongside a substitute from the other team. The two approach the lane line, and immediately I flinch at first sight of him. I'm startled seeing him here, the substituting opponent: *Simeon*.

The terror from that spine-chilling night begins replaying in my head.

"One more," says the ref, delivering the ball for my second shot.

There he is. Like, right there. *Alive,* and supposedly, since he's on this court and playing again, healthy too. I look at him carefully without knowing what to say. He glances back, so I continue staring — a stunned, thorough gaze at this ghost appearing right before my eyes. My thoughts race with confusion, wondering whether he recovered from that night some years ago or if he still relives the trauma in his nightmares.

Simeon turns away then looks at me again. A cold glare this time, a disdainful glare. He untucks his jersey and casually reveals the gruesome scar across his midsection. "Wounds heal," he utters. "You gonna shoot or what?"

I'm shocked, staggered. *Am I gonna shoot? Did he just ask that?* I mean, it's not like I'm troubled for trivial reasons, like his stab wound needed only a Band-Aid and some ointment. Just by looking at him, I can still hear the slash to his flesh, echoes of the shrieks and screams. The thought that that could've been me still sends goosebumps down my neck. *My bad, Simeon. That night didn't almost ruin or end my life as I knew it. What do you mean, 'am I gonna shoot?' Are you gonna tell me how you're doing later, or why I even was Jame's target to be slain? Hell, is he here in the stands too?*

"How much time's he get!" Simeon blurts, defying all the concerns shooting through my mind.

The ref reacts, "Get the shot off!"

I hurriedly bounce the ball twice or so without even thinking of my routine, that tranquil memory of Woolner Park now replaced by my worst experience there. Nonetheless, second shot — *swish*. My first two points of the tournament; forget game or quarter. It's obvious I'm off to a slow start, but it's a start at least.

I dart back for a last-second stint of defense, then to the bench as the third quarter ends. Discreetly eyeing Pop in the bleachers, I notice there's doubt painted all over his face. *Is he embarrassed? Did I fail him?* He wears the same look that Feldbrook would give me after I'd unload a jumble of excuses to justify my self-pity.

I twist open a cool lemon-lime Gatorade and sip it a few times, focused on Feldbrook's advice looping in my head: *failure is only a figment of one's mind...*

Two points in almost four games isn't nearly worth any celebration, but it's where I encounter a pivotal fork along this journey.

I could cut my losses and accept two points, then bail out for the fourth quarter and contemplate flaking on tomorrow's gold- or bronze-medal game, with some lame excuse like, *You guys are better off without me*, or, *Something came up, fellas — I got somewhere to be in the morning.*

I could walk out carrying my duffle bag over my shoulder with the pocket-sized remains of my pride, hoping to put this weekend behind me as soon as possible. I could even try convincing myself that Hoops 'n Hearts is just a meaningless charity tourney, despite knowing it's not.

Or I could veer onto a different route.

I could use these two points as the first step toward rediscovering the belief, the conviction, the confidence I once had. Pop is not embarrassed, and I am not failing him. Even if he is, and even if I am, it wouldn't matter.

Because *I* decide when I fail, which occurs only when *I* stop shooting, when *I* stop trying, when *I* cower and defer, when *I* bow down to adversity.

I could use these two points as inspiration for four points, then six, and build on these meagre milestones to guide myself in the right direction.

Again, Feldbrook, wherever he is ... he is here, with me. I've come too far even to think of giving up this time. *Head in the game, Udoka.*

* * *

We trail 62–59 with little time remaining in the fourth quarter.

I'm parked on the sideline by the scorer's table, awaiting the substitution horn and what could be the final window of redemption for my broken athletic career. Keele, who's been dominating all game with his gritty in-your-face defense and timely baskets when we needed one, fouls out with twenty-one seconds left.

I holler his name, pointing at him for his attention. Keele hangs his head, looking defeated. I don't know if he's moping about getting disqualified or if he's worried that I, of the few on the bench, have elected to check in for the game's most crucial moment. Regardless, I shout, "I got you!"

He takes a lengthy look over my shoulder at the scoreboard, panting heavily.

"No," Keele responds, tugging away at his tucked-in jersey. He pounds his fist against my chest and looks at me fixedly. "Not me," he says. "You got *us*."

Surprised and without an affirmative response, I nod back and make my way onto the floor.

Both teams await the whistle for a frontcourt sideline inbound as I take on Keele's match-up: Simeon, who'd only played meaningful minutes in the fourth quarter and was pedestrian initially but began heating up in the game's final minutes. He presents a slender frame that is easily misconstrued as a weak trait; and for that, Keele made the mistake of pressing into him and playing the enforcer, the bully, the intimidator. So Simeon, using several tactics to exaggerate petty contact, has capitalized whenever we got overzealous. And when we were, he gladly strolled to the line to shoot free throws as our guys bickered with a ref or sulked on the bench in foul trouble. Keele could attest — he's punching air right now.

As the whistle blows, Simeon sprints up the sideline and toward the inbounder after using a pin-down screen. I'm playing with fire as I trail him — aware of his flopping schemes and the touchy fouls that have been called — though I still chase closely, tugging at his shorts. I'm not holding him much, but it's just enough to slow him down.

We both chase after the ball while it floats to where the centreline and sideline meet, as Simeon, cornered by the two, spreads his hands to receive it. I swipe for a deflection, batting the ball off Simeon's knee and out of bounds before he even lays a fingertip on it.

"That's us, ref!" I plead.

"Off him!" Simeon rebuts.

The ref blows the whistle. "Out of bounds! Goin' the other way!" he calls as roars arise from our bench.

Marr finds me open on the following play as I sprint along the baseline from the right corner to the left. Simeon guards me closely, one hand tracing my fakes, the other pressing my ribcage. I jab to my left then feint to shoot as Simeon's stance begins to unsettle. I take a convincing drive toward the basket then spin away from traffic and into the lane. Scoot drifts to the weak-side corner and shows his ready hands for a catch-and-shoot three-pointer, but I see his defender lurking and luring me into what could be an intercepted pass.

So, I take flight underneath the basket, dipping my shoulder into their tall, lanky centre's body. High above the rim, he extends both of his wiry-long arms to contest my shot, so I cradle Her in my right hand, contorting midair to evade the defender for a scoop shot that kisses the top of the glass. The ball circles the rim before softly falling through the mesh as I tumble to the floor.

62–61. Nine seconds left. Down one.

Simeon is smothered in his backcourt by the air-tight double team of Marr and Scoot while I quickly gather myself up off the hardwood, trailing the play, hollering to them, "Stay in the trap, Scoot!" and, "Marr, I got yours!"

The menacing pair leads Simeon, again, cornered into the same sideline near midcourt. Marr's man flails his arms aloft, hoping to be seen while he's open — and he is, but only for an instant as I hustle to cover his area. Simeon rids himself of the swarming ball pressure and chucks a lobbed pass to his distant teammate.

I can feel the revived crowd gasp as the ball's in the air. I can feel Simeon's hopes of a near-perfect fourth quarter hanging in the balance of a dangerous cross-court pass. I can feel the thrill of landing a fingertip on the ball as it gets deflected into the open court, and the relief of chasing it down. *This is it. This is the big play. I've made the big play*!

I race down the vacant court against the game's dying seconds, envisioning myself as though I'm watching me from the stands, next to Pop or whomever. It feels like everything is unraveling in slow-motion, like the play-by-play is heard by my ears only:

"*Clendon gets a hand on the ball*! *He's all alone … four seconds … three … two … will he beat the buzzerrr*?"

My feet leave the floor.

I raise the ball above my head with my eyes on Her home, and I feel — for once in several trying years — how it feels to fly again. Not jump — *fly*. Fly as I did when I was a child, where I'd weave through an imaginary defense before soaring with the pros, pretending I could hang in the air for as long as they could. I'm flying! Well above the rim; well above my anxieties and fears that have been shackling me to the floor.

The clock ticks down, but not before I flip the ball into the cylinder and have Her sweep past the soft twine. The buzzer sounds and the crowd cheers from behind me. I abruptly land on my feet, feeling a sharp ache surging from my right knee to every point in my body.

Crick-crack! it goes.

But I'm numb to it.

Nothing can remove me from this out-of-body experience. *I'm flying, Pop*! I'm flying again, with no plan of coming back down.

Final score: 63–62.

Championship's tomorrow.

* * *

The house is dim and still when I twiddle my key into the front door. Ma's a few hours into her night shift. Leena's probably at Ella's or keeping her word to at least show her face at "that Saturday-night shindig in some kid from school's musty basement," she called it. She's not into parties or the underage boozing — which is curious because she's a social butterfly otherwise. "I'll celebrate after my big break," she often tells me, whenever I insist she lighten up and think about something other than her hopeful acting career. I suppose I had the same idea when

I was her age. And as I drop my duffel bag by the entrance and flick on the nearest light switch, this feels much the same as it was years ago too: dragging myself into the kitchen after a late-night game, wondering whether I shot the ball well or defended poorly or whatever.

That postgame loneliness. It revisits me.

Bzzz! Bzzz!

There goes Mo, being her supportive self as always. She knew exactly how I felt coming into this weekend: iffy, full of jitters, foreign to this game that used to come so natural to me. I want to be free from her concern this time.

I lock my phone then slip it into my sweatpants.

Bzzz! *Bzzz*! it goes again. I feel my teeth grinding together, my nostrils flaring. *Ah, c'mon, Mo. I'm fine, I said!*

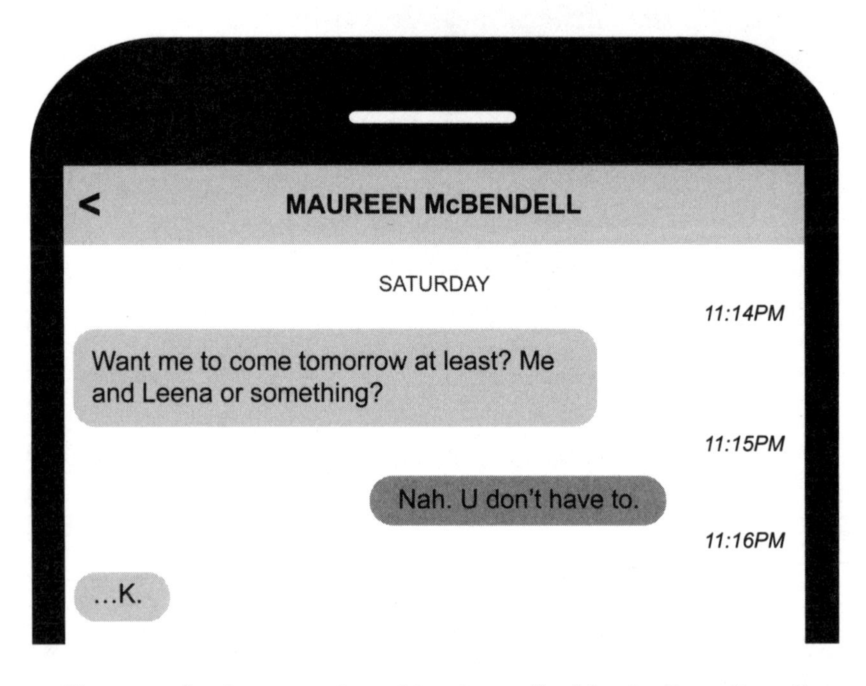

I'm caught by surprise this time. Suddenly I realize I haven't been deprived of the postgame chit-chat with Ma or Leena, or even as recently with Mo — because it's always been nonexistent with them, which I've also realized is completely fine and was already fine to begin with. Because I've longed for Pop's reactions, Pop's two cents. Not theirs. Not anyone else's — *Pop's.*

I slide down the wall in the kitchen, clutching my phone.

SATURDAY

Pop
Had to leave ASAP after your game. My bad. Way to throw down tonight tho. Great game! See u tomorrow. Get some rest. OK...out! *11:16PM*

I catch myself gazing into the distance. Seeing Pop's text reminds me of how much I used to cherish the postgame talks with him, even when he would make me fret, because they occurred at a time when basketball fulfilled me. I think about the full-of-life kid I once was, with my hands tarred and ashy from an afternoon of hoops at Woolner Park; or during high school, when my sneakers eroded at the soles was proof of time well spent along the hardwood of a gym like Oakwood's. I fed my blood, sweat, and tears into this elusive, unfulfilled dream of playing hoops at the highest levels.

Though here I sit, my feet numb to the cold kitchen floor, my knee purple and swollen and tucked snugly against my chest, realizing it was not a dream I was chasing all these years but a tenacious pursuit of becoming the best version of *me* that I can be.

Images from the semis constantly replay. I see the regret on Simeon's face as he threw the ball away; the hoop as I rose for the game-winning flush; the pandemonium of the crowd after the buzzer sounded and how my teammates flooded the floor to embrace me.

That moment was earned.

The struggles and bruises and doubts and injuries and hardships and the thousands upon thousands of lonely hours dedicated to the game at Woolner Park and Oakwood and Carinci and in the McInnis Centre and everywhere else, were not at all dues paid in vain. Because they all led me here, toward *my moment.*

It's mine forever.

I glide my thumb across the screen to reopen the message thread. The fear, the angst, the mental toll of performing my best, in front of Pop, for Pop — the worries that have troubled me — they all seep out from the depths of my lungs with the air I exhale.

A calm grin begins to form. My thumbs tap gently against the screen:

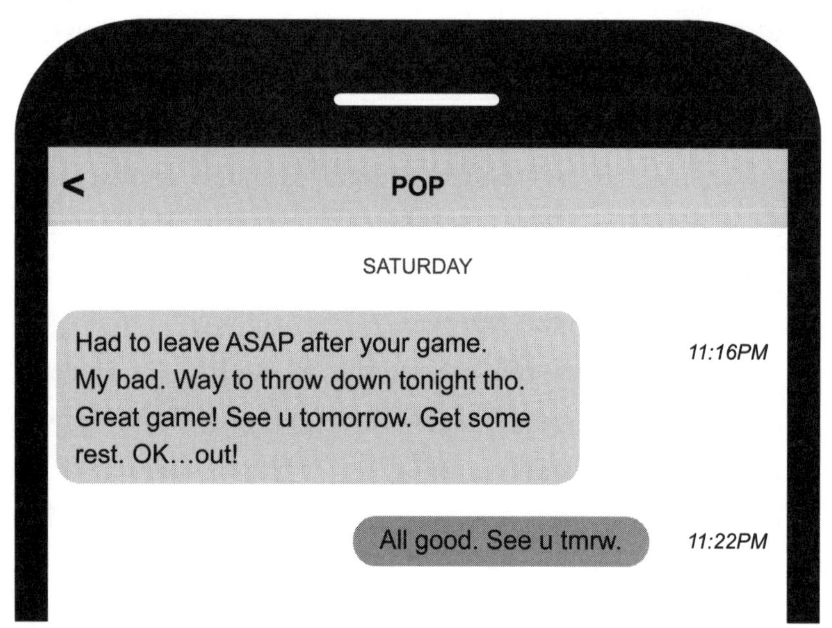

CHAPTER XVIII

WHAT GOES UP

Beads of sweat trickle down my face when I stare into the spirited championship Sunday crowd. Keele looks ready, so does Marr. Goose and Scoot, too. They seem focused, determined; and although Pop is nowhere to be found in these bleachers, so am I. He'll get here when he gets here. In the meantime, *let's go*! *Let's get this damn thing going*!

The whistle is blown; the ball is tossed gently in the air. Scoot reaches the ceiling to win us the championship game's first possession.

Marr dribbles steadily into the frontcourt. Sprinting to the baseline, I can feel a throb in my knee after every stride. Keele plants his feet for a sturdy down-screen, allowing me to break free of my defender along the wing. "See me open!" I holler, ready to make a play the moment She's in my hands.

Marr crosses over and delivers a bounce pass to my shooting pocket. I set my feet with my knees bent, then I raise and fire. Those same early-game jitters from years ago, from yesterday morning, even — they must've tampered with my touch, because the ball feels real funny leaving my hands. She might even skip against the backboard and miss the basket completely. Yup, She does, landing nearly out-of-bounds where Scoot hustles to save Her from heading into the stands.

Damnit.

I remember when I'd hide in the baseline corner after missing a shot badly. It was like I had blown my chance to score and didn't deserve another one until everyone watching forgot about it. All these flashes from the past when I'd cower — they're behind me. They race through my mind and enrage me. *Shoot again.*

"Right back here!" I holler.

Scoot pivots around, doing all he can to avoid a double team. He spins in the direction of my voice then slings the ball from above his head to where I've relocated behind the perimeter. I set my feet again and rise for another try. This time, She flows to the basket with perfect aim, perfect arc, perfect rotation. I let my wrist hang while I wait. *Nothing but net.*

On defense, Keele pesters the ballhandler up the

court and forces an early pass to my man. I gamble for the go-ahead steal but miss the ball, so Marr covers me for help defense. Recovering into the play, I hurry to Marr's matchup, who is left open for a baseline jumper, and although I'm late contesting the shot, the ball rattles off the side of the rim and bounces my way for an easy loose-ball rebound.

I'm dribbling up the court, weaving between defenders as they reach for the ball. Keele leaks down the floor and calls for a pass. "Cutter!" he shouts, as I zip the ball through traffic. The bounce pass leads Keele to the basket, where he flips a shot off the top of the square. The ball skips around the hoop then lands through the mesh. We're off to a 5–0 lead in the opening minute of action. Dashing back on defense, I smack my hands together, feeling pumped about my early start.

"Good dish!" Keele exclaims, reaching for a high-five before we part ways. I witness the applauding crowd, my cheering teammates on the bench rising to their feet, the finger-pointing opponents in shambles and on the brink of an early timeout — and I think to myself: I am *exactly* where I've always wanted to be.

I'm present. I'm absorbed in the moment, and this moment only.

Feldbrook was right: moments are what you make of them. *You* determine the moments that matter from the ones that don't. *You* determine what is real to your heart and what isn't. And this moment, right here, through the lens of my hopeful eyes, is so scenic and fulfilling and like none other from the past few years. This moment is everything.

I take it all in and embrace this moment like it's my last.

* * *

Somewhere in the stands, I'm sure he's here, watching me thrive. He'd been so adamant about numbers ever since I began playing organized ball. He'd ask me, *Are you counting your points as you run up and down the floor? How many shots did you get off? How many boards have you pulled down so far?* To answer what I'm sure he's been wondering: *No; I'm not sure; and a few, so far, I guess. I don't know, Pop.*

I'm not worrying about any of that. I did score a bunch, though. I caught my defender sleeping off a backdoor cut for an easy two, midway through the first quarter. I knocked down a few triples in the first half and sank another pair right after halftime. My defender kept sagging off me like I hadn't been red-hot all game. So, shoot I did — willingly and without hesitation.

I've been picking apart the defense in pick-and-rolls too. *Take what the defense gives you,* Pop used to tell me. And I've been doing just that. Surgically. If they blitzed the screen, I'd dump a pocket pass to my screener or swing it to my weak-side shooter for an open shot. If they played the screen soft, I'd either set myself up for an easy jumper, attack the basket for a score, or dish it out to whoever was open. And when they had the audacity to switch one of their bigs onto me, oh, my eyes would just light up! I'd score on each of those flat-footed, clumsy giants they threw at me. Every. Single. Time.

I've also been having a field day at the line. Whenever they'd come too close, I'd absorb the contact then stroll to the charity stripe to sink a pair. I couldn't tell you how many I made, but I don't remember missing on any of them.

Now, how many points might that be? From the quick tally in my head: *enough.* Enough to keep my foot pressed on the gas, fearlessly. And right now, I'm flooring it with dense lead boots.

As for my rebounds, my assists, my steals, what have you — I couldn't begin to guess those numbers. But I'm in all the right places at the right times, making all the right plays to help my team win.

I'm living in the moment, you see.

My moment. I'm here. I'm present, Pop. You should be proud.

* * *

A minute and eleven seconds remain, and the score is deadlocked at seventy-three apiece. A timeout has been called, so the team is hovering over Keele as he traces what seems to be a half-court trap on the palm of his hand. He shouts, "Be ready when they cross half-court, fellas! Not the first, but on the second pass — that's our cue to pounce on 'em!"

"Got it," says Marr.

"I'm with you." Scoot nods.

"Imma be dead centre at midcourt," Keele continues. "Yoosie, Marr, you two cover the sidelines. Whichever side they dribble on, I'll come trap 'em with one of you. Whoever's left, you gotta rotate to the middle to cover me. Get ready for that big steal! Scoot, Goose — stay on your toes and protect home. Got that?"

"Yeah, Keele!"

"Cool."

"Heard you!"

"Yessir! Let's get it!"

Keele shouts, "Win on two!" He raises his fist above his head as we gather in. "One ... two..."

"Win!"

The other team's point guard strolls across his backcourt and flings a pass to the sideline, where Marr immediately hounds the new ballhandler. Keele lurks amid the action and for an instant is steady, then he scrambles to Marr's sideline for the harassing double-team as planned. Toward the top of the arc, I rush to cover Keele's man, but with a keen eye not only on my matchup, but on the ball as well.

Someone hollers: "Loose ball!"

I turn and see Her skipping across the open court near me.

"That's your steal, Yoos!" Keele exclaims, urging me to hustle before the ball goes out of bounds. I spill to the floor, though I'm not alone. From out of nowhere comes an opponent about to take a dive.

He tosses himself to the floor.

His body clips my legs from under me, the weight of maybe two hundred pounds colliding full force and head-on.

Snap!

The sound emanates to all corners of the gym, causing a crowd-wide gasp.

My knee.

No. *No, no, no, no*!

My … my knee! My precious friggin' knee!

"*Arghhhhhhhh*!"

A horrid silence sucks the air from the gym. In a blink, I see jumbles of people. Players. Spectators. Medical staff rushing to me with giant bags of ice and Saran wrap. I feel their feet thudding against the hardwood. They flood the court where I lie screaming and writhing and pounding my fists on the floor.

But you — where are you? Where the hell are you!

My eyes scrunch as though grimacing could ease the pain. I see yesterday's game-winning steal and slam after the dreadful games I had before, the dreadful *years* I had before. I see your "*Great game*" text and relive the joy I felt just a night ago, the elation of wrapping my head around playing in front of you one last time. I mourn the bliss of what it felt like to fly again. Those clouds, they were lovely. They were everything.

The pain spreads from my knee; I can feel it in every inch in my body with just a minor budge of my leg. Here on this cold floor, I'm reminded that gravity is a force not to be messed with — because those clouds, those lovely clouds, they're no longer upon me. They escape me and disappear into a figment of nothing.

"Yoosie..." I hear faintly. It's Keele's voice. "I'm ... I'm sorry," he says, his eyes reddened and watery.

I'm delirious, unsure how to respond.

Keele kneels by my side. He's overtaken by a tremble in his chest, a hoarsening in his voice. "I shouldn't've—"

"Shouldn't've ... shouldn't've what?" I ask him, feeling my eyelids closing together.

"I — I..." Keele stutters. "This wouldn't've happened if I ... if I didn't..."

He morphs into a fuzzy figure and is consumed by the darkness before my eyes.

CHAPTER XIX
MONTHS LATER
I AM WHO?

Sunlight rushes in between the blinds by the windowsill. It floods the room with broad, bright stripes that contrast with the shadows across my skin, across the furniture, across the four walls that cage me. These four walls, grey and bare — they have become my solitude.

It's been about a week since I last invited the sun in here; since I last felt reason to leave my bed and venture outside of these four walls for anything more than a basic interaction or something to keep my stomach from growling.

I've yet to decide whether getting back to my life before the injury could do any good. Seeing people, going out again — that sort of thing. I don't care to see or talk to anyone. Not Mo. Not Ma or Leena. Not Keele or Feldbrook, and certainly not Pop. Not a single soul.

Because my knee *still* hurts.

Badly. Really, really badly.

I mean, sure, soon I'll have to return to normalcy, but it all seems so daunting.

For instance, there's post-op rehab. And, oh how I despise every moment of it. Holding on to the false hope of a quick and easy recovery — it's been a drag. All I can do is "be patient" and buy into my doctor's "clinical expertise."

The look on Dr. Kasie's face still plagues me, the time she ripped open the curtains to my hospital bed right after the injury. She had cheerful eyes and a lift in her cheeks, which wasn't easily construed as a smile but was certainly disturbing given the fate of my knee.

"It's confirmed! You've suffered what's called the unhappy triad," she exclaimed without the slightest regret. I must've looked stunned, baffled, maybe — the way she so eagerly volunteered some info: "It's a complete tear of the meniscus. The ACL and MCL too. That is, the anterior cru—"

"I know what they are!" I snapped. Mo sat bedside, her hands folded into mine, trying to ease my despair.

And just when I thought Dr. Kasie had ripped off the bandage, there she was with that oblivious look on her face, rubbing salt on the wound.

"How's your head feeling, Mister Clendon?" she asked, clearing her throat. "You took quite a spill."

I nodded, glaring sharply at her.

Wincing ever so slightly, she added, "You've also suffered a grade two concussion."

Lovely, Dr. Kasie. Superb, I thought.

When I asked how long I'd be out for, she advised I "stay away from screens, loud noises, and bright lights until reassessment," as though I'd willingly get around in heavily tinted sunglasses and earplugs again! As for my knee, I gulped when Dr. Kasie broke the news to me: "Pending immediate surgery, it'll be good as new by," — she stared blankly, working out a timeline — "the first week of March. If you rehab it well, that is."

* * *

I felt hopeful, despite accepting that I had no intention of ever dribbling a basketball again — which is still true. *Even still — newsflash, Dr. Kasie: today marks a whole six weeks after the first week of March, a near eternity since my precious knee was sliced and implanted with the new parts that you said would heal me. The migraines still come and go, too.*

And still I stare out into the overcast sky, drowning in self-pity.

Though as I look outside through the window, I realize that a blade of sunlight still found me in my darkness. And within that narrow gleam of light, there is still solace to all my pains; hopefulness in all my doubts; and some clarity in who I think I am.

There's a silver lining out there. It's bright. It's promising. It's a glimpse of hope.

I've been given heaps of free time. Time to think. Time to let my mind to slip into the many what-ifs I've made conscious efforts to ignore: *What if I didn't take that dive? What if I dove a second earlier? What if I cut in on Keele during that timeout and suggested a basic 2-3 zone instead of the half-court trap he had wanted? What if I just said 'no' to Pop, to Keele, when asked to play? What might've panned out for me?*

Well, I'd be walking without a limp and thinking without a headache, that's for sure.

Because, yeah, my knee still hurts, and splintering migraines still surge and split my brain into a thousand tiny pieces. But if I didn't play, I wouldn't have found closure in this lifelong quest of figuring out who I am — with or without Her in my life. I wouldn't have finally faced and conquered my obstacles head-on, all the while burdened with the fears, the doubts. You see, I'm grateful for the aches, the nagging voice in my head telling me I shouldn't've taken that dive — because these petty little what-ifs are nothing compared to the regret I would've faced had I never walked into that gym. So, I'm glad I did, because another bellringer and a sick knee came at the expense of the most fulfilling moment of my life.

And I can live with that.

* * *

Leena taps against my bedroom door and barges in before I can work up a reaction.

"Coming in!" she exclaims. "With good news!"

"Like what's the point of knocking nowadays, right?"

"Ah, shut it!" She dives onto my bed and engulfs me in a gleeful embrace. Whatever's up better be worth this energy. She snags one of the open envelopes from under my phone. "Ugh! What's with you and these letters?"

"Give it back!"

"If there's another girl, I won't be the one to break it to Mo. That's all you, bro!" she teases.

I rip the envelope from her hand. "You don't know nothin'."

"Wrong! You see, I know that you've had your secret admirer, or pen pal or whatever, for years now. I know that it's creepy. I know that nowadays, *normal* people use these super-cool, handheld computer-thingies that let you talk and send — I dunno — texts and emails and DMs so that you could chat with other normal people," she jeers, as though my iPhone isn't resting right there on my nightstand.

"Is that all?"

"Nope! I know you've been hibernating in this little man-cave for way too long. There's like, a stench in here now." I scowl at her. "I mean, don't you have one of your basketball friends to hang out with?"

"Nope."

"Any parties?"

"Nope."

"You and Mo in a rough patch?"

"Why are you in my room?"

"Got something to tell you!" She's aware of my gloomy mood but unwilling to stoop down to it. "I signed my first role! I'm gonna be this lawyer's brainiac niece on this crime show! Landed a couple lines in this one scene..."

I feel my eyes widen, seeing a glow in Leena's cheeks as she babbles about this new opportunity. My thoughts trace back to the Leena I knew some years ago: the Leena who hadn't yet found her calling but whose smile would still light up any room in the same way; the Leena who endured through a dark and seemingly endless tunnel but knew a glimpse of light would appear at some point; the Leena who embraced her journey because she loved her art and cherished the process of putting one foot in front of the other, no matter how long the tunnel might have seemed or how many people might have discouraged her from carrying on.

Gazing deeper into Leena's glimmering eyes, I'm staring at the living proof of everything Feldbrook taught me.

"It's a pilot episode," she continues. "So there's potential for something huge ... Oh! And during my audition, the producers were even chatting about a movie spin-off, maybe!"

"Wow, Leena. This is ... this is amazing."

"Right!"

"I'm so, so proud of you."

"*Eeek*! I know!" She grabs my hands and squeezes them tightly. "Now come out for lunch to celebrate me! It'll be me and my friends and a few other cast members!"

"I mean, I dunno."

"C'mon. Please?"

"Ahh, fine."

"Stop being a grouch!" Leena rips the sheets off my bed and scurries out into the hallway. "You're coming!" she hollers. "Starts at two forty-five!"

I wriggle gingerly to the edge of my bed, doing everything to keep my knee from moving — wincing whenever it bends. I mean, fine. I can't stay cooped up in here forever. I'll go.

Ding! *Ding*! *Ding*!

The jingle startles me. I haven't heard from or reached out to anyone in weeks.

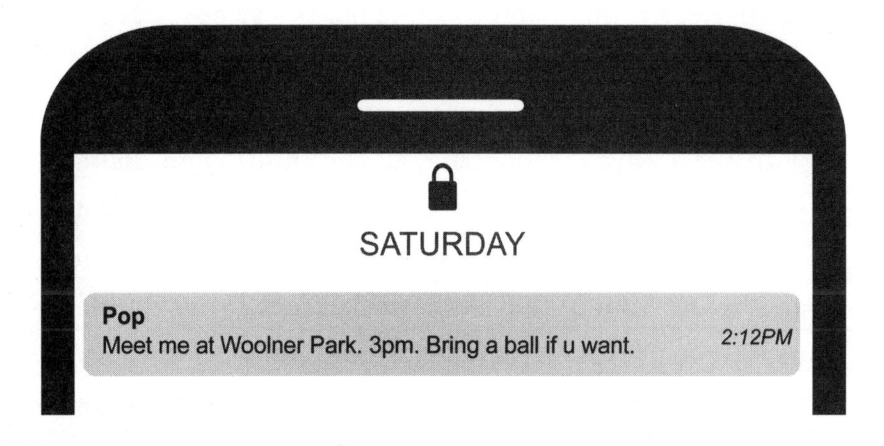

Damn. "Oh, Leena! Wait, come back! Leena!"

"*Whaaat*," she calls from the bathroom, "I'm getting ready!" Leena treads heavily to my room, splotches of foundation dabbed on her forehead, a powder brush clenched between her teeth. She tugs at her flashy blouse until it fits comfortably. "What is it? Why aren't you up yet!"

"Something came up." I grimace. "Can't come."

"*Ughhh*!" She stomps. "Seriously?"

I nod regretfully.

"Fine! Whatever."

"I wanna say congrats, though."

"Yeah, cool. Thanks." Leena begins pacing back to the bathroom, swishing light swirls of makeup along her cheeks.

"No, seriously! Wait up, now!" She turns back around, crossing her arms with her sassy self. "I know what it's like chasing a dream. Working toward something that seems nearly impossible at some point. I've been caught up with basketball all this time and hadn't always been there to check up on how you were doing. Y'know — with the acting, the dancing, all the theatre and drama stuff. So, I can't say I knew exactly what it took for you to land a gig, but I'm sure it took a lot. A lot of courage and belief. A lot of soul-searching. A lot of ignoring the naysayers. Heaps of passion, I bet, and obviously ten times the hard work, too." I look at her tenderly, feeling a smile form. "I can learn a thing or two from you, lil' sis. I'm so happy for you."

"Oh…" Leena says, trying to hide her reciprocated affection. She and I have dodged plenty of mushy sibling moments growing up, though she can't help but smile back this time. "Thank you."

"Enjoy lunch with your crew. Kill it on-set."

"Ha! 'Kill it, *bro*! Hundred and ten percent!'" she mocks. "Locker room talk, it's funny. In Hollywood they say, 'Break a leg.'"

"Now how'd that come about?"

She shrugs. "Not sure. Some way of saying, 'Good luck.'"

I look at her curiously then glance at my knee. "Well, all right. Break a leg then! Just don't tear your ACL!"

* * *

Hobbling downstairs, I can hear the TV flipping through channels. I'm caught by the sound of cheery jingles from possibly a game show. An intense, cello-based score from what could be a cheesy soap opera. A forecast of *heavy showers leading into the evening*. Ma's downstairs, I bet. And the swishing sound of water running from the kitchen faucet makes me certain it's her, because Leena's allergic to washing dishes.

Ma peeks out into the hallway and finds me approaching. She must've heard my heavy feet clunking to the floor. "How're you feeling, darling?" she asks, a soapy plate clutched in one hand, the remote converter in the other.

"I'm fine, Ma. Gotta head out soon."

"Great! Celebrating Leena's big break?"

"Nah. I was going to. But not anymore."

"Oh. Well, where're you off to?"

"The park."

I watch her eyes wander to the basketball I'm clutching at my waist; she's giving me this dubious look.

"My knee's fine, Ma," I assure her. "Just gonna shoot around, nothing crazy."

"Have you eaten today? I can make something."

"I'll be fine," I reply, limping to the fridge, jerking open its door for something quick and already prepped. No luck — it's crammed with raw produce, bottled juices, and slabs of seasoned meat marinating under a tight seal. There's gotta be *something.* On the top shelf are a near-dozen eggs in an open carton and soggy greens that I promised to finish earlier in the week before they'd turn mushy. Below I find a couple Granny Smiths, plump with their stems. "I'll grab an apple or whatever. But thanks, Ma."

"Well ... okay."

Officials continue to move aggressively on the reopened case for a missing Jameis McBendell...

My stomach twists.

Better known as Jame, McBendell was last seen playing basketball at Woolner Park, minutes from Jane Street and St. Clair Avenue, around four years ago. As the result of an alleged altercation before his last sighting, anonymous witnesses corroborated McBendell's involvement in the past scuffle, leading to his disappearance. During that time, officials investigated the premises of Woolner Park and its surroundings, including nearby regions of Black Creek between Jane Street and Rockcliffe Boulevard, but to no avail — until years later from then and several months ago, buried near this trail behind me, just walking distance north of Woolner Park, a silver necklace with a round medallion was found. Acquaintances of McBendell's were troubled and shaken, confirming the necklace had belonged to him based on the medallion's distinct inscriptions...

I feel my heart pounding. Everything surrounding me seems to disappear as I'm drawn in by the sight of the TV, the voice of the reporter.

And for today's breaking news, just this morning — from what has been a multi-year, needle-in-a-haystack investigation — detectives have retrieved further evidence potentially related to McBendell's disappearance: a set of longnose pliers — found, again, here at Black Creek — dug up just a matter of footsteps from where the necklace was initially hidden.

"Longnose pliers?" Ma reacts.

"Shhh!"

Officials have their eyes set on a suspect but continue to request info from the public, considering all potential leads with considerable caution, given the lengthy timeline from the date of McBendell's vanishing. Forensic investigators are uncertain whether fingerprints are identifiable at this time.

The screen goes blank and the room silent. I look at Ma; she looks at me with her thumb pressed on the remote converter. "That's … that's enough," she murmurs.

Bzzz! Bzzz!

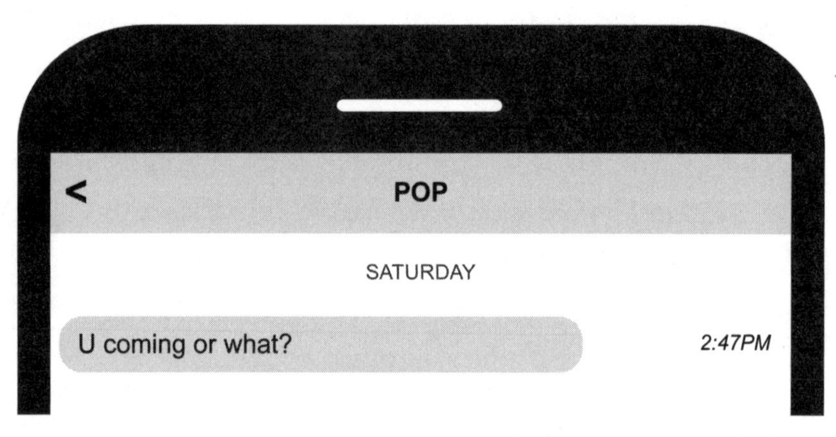

I'm shuddering at all the signs, all the clues to which I've been blind. My hand quivers as I grab my phone.

Heading out. Be there in 10 2:48PM

CHAPTER XX

COME AGAIN ANOTHER DAY

It's curious how I'm relying again on basketball for distraction when She's the last thing I want on my mind. But I need Her right now, because I can't shake what I just watched: caution tape surrounding the crime scene, just minutes away from *here*, the place where I spent my childhood; the news reporter behind the "*MISSING MAN*" headline — this all can't be real.

I'm twirling the ball in my hands, all for whatever can put me at ease. It's been a while since the last time I was here. I sat on this same picnic bench many years ago, being introduced to Her and Her to me.

Children are frolicking in the spring breeze under dark, gathering clouds that threaten a downpour. They sweep their feet across the restored blacktop; it's got a dope layout now, with these *massive* turquoise and salmon block letters sharing the court with crisp, white boundaries and lane lines. I was thrilled just taking in the new look when I got here, let alone understanding it, but catching a far-enough view, I'm able to make out what it says: *CHOOSE TO SHINE*.

I'm hoping these kids will do just that — *shine*, and not have any doubts or worries or fears whenever they're dribbling the rock. And with Woolner Park's fresh makeover, including these brand-new nets and glassy backboards, these kids should be all right. I still envision my younger self in them. I was these kids once upon a time, playing pickup against friends and strangers until the hoops disappeared with the sun.

"There you are," I hear from a distance. It's Pop.

I strap on my knee brace and dribble onto the court. The children start vacating after hearing the rim clank from my first shot. My knee's killing me, but I shoot again, single-legged, missing off the back end of the rim. Next shot — in-and-out. She takes a bounce or two under the basket then begins rolling away.

"Still won't chase after your shot, huh? Ain't nothin' changed," Pop teases.

Well, I suppose he's right. Thinking back to how I've struggled with keeping the ball in my court, here he is, fetching after my rebound.

"Guess not," I respond. "Just like—"

"Old times." He's hesitant to embrace me, though he does so anyway.

"How've you been, Pop?"

"Surviving," he says, tossing me the ball. "You went on a tear in the championship game, months back! Y'know, that charity thing?"

A tear. Fitting.

"Yeah. You must've heard," I say, giving him a cold scowl. "My knee did, too. I was only out there so you could watch me play again."

"I knew you wouldn't wanna play, man. Had to give your boy a few bucks to convince you. I thought he had a better shot at it than me. And I was right. What's it — Kean, or Cole or something?"

"Keele!" I shout, delivering a crisp chest pass. If the ball jams his finger, or skips his hands and strikes his chest, then hey, so be it. "You're lucky I played. I promised I would, remember? I honour my promises."

"So that makes you all *noble* now, huh," he jeers, flipping the ball back at me. "Who taught you that nonsense?"

"Not *who*. *What*. And even if I wanted a lesson on nobility or keeping my word or whatever, rest assured you wouldn't be teaching it."

"Uh-huh. So, *what,* then?"

I kiss my teeth. "Forget it, man."

"Nah, speak!"

Drawing in a shallow breath, I'm hoping whatever I'm about to say won't escape me, because I need Pop to *feel* the hurt he'd caused.

"It's the pain of feeling lost with this hoops thing for as long as I can remember. Searching high and low for its meaning and then *finally* realizing what it's all about for me — just for you to miss every moment of it. Wanting to share that feeling, that joy with *you* again, in that final charity game, and all for nothing. *That* taught me a lot."

Pop takes his time responding. "Udoka … I'm … I'm sorry. But why'd I wanna see you lay helplessly on the floor like that, anyway?" He grimaces. "Screaming in all that pain I heard you were in…"

"I've been through worse. Yeah, blowing out my knee took a toll. My head taking a spill — sure, wasn't fun. But wailing on that floor, looking into the crowd near and far, left and right, not for a trainer, not for first aid, but for you — *you*! And to learn you weren't even there? *That* was painful. Thinking back on all I've been through, struggling with prep school in the States and with college ball up here too … then delivering my finest hour since my Oakwood days, the only time in *years* I could truly admit to feeling like myself on the court … just to realize the only person I wanted watching me play wasn't around. That *hurt*. Far worse than any snap of the leg or blow to the head."

"I should've been there."

"But like you said, I guess I *am* noble. I oughta be noble. Noble enough to forgive. Noble enough to forget."

I take a few dribbles before tossing a bounce pass for a game of one-on-one, just like how it used to be, so I can close this chapter of my life with what had initially opened the book. One last game against Pop — not as my greatest critic or cheerleader or coach from the bleachers, but *Pop*.

"You ... gotta know something..." he mutters, as though he wished I hadn't heard him.

"Know *what*?"

Pop parks himself along the sideline, expecting me to join.

"I–I've come to say ... goodbye, Udoka."

"Goodbye?"

"Goodbye."

I can feel my teeth grinding, my heart pounding. I'm standing on the blacktop with its painted lines, both straight and round. He knows I heard him but won't dare repeat what he said.

"Check up," I demand.

He doesn't budge.

I repeat: "Check! Check the damn ball, man!"

Still nothing.

"Your knee," Pop says. "You know you can't play."

"So, what, *now* you wanna keep me from getting hurt? What about all those years when I wondered where you were? When you'd come back? Where was your concern back then, huh? Now you wanna care?"

"You know that ain't the case."

"I don't think I do, *Pierce*."

He's drawn aback. "You wouldn't understand. It's just better this way."

"Check the ball, or I'm outta here! That's what you want, anyway — me outta your life again, like old times, right?" He remains on the ground, so I turn away and give the ball a bounce, letting out some frustration.

"Wait," he goes. I turn back and find him looking sharply into my troubled eyes. "I don't got much time left here. I'm ... I'm truly sorry, Udoka." He reaches into his pocket, unraveling what seems to be a wrinkly pamphlet with his handwriting on it.

"What, another stupid charity tournament you want me playing in? What's next, Pop, my ankle this time?"

"C'mon, take it! I scrambled finding something to write on. It's just a letter! Please," he begs, forcing it onto me. "It'll be the last thing I ask of you. You need this, before I go."

"Nah. I'm good with that." I shove his hand aside, but he jostles for my pockets, so I shove him harder and strike him away from me.

His eyes gape wide, as though he's surprised I'm

retaliating. "Eh, watch it!" he warns, sticking a finger in my face. "You forget why they call me 'Pop,' huh? I don't care if you're my lil' brother. You could still get popped in the jaw just like the rest of 'em did back then! Back when I did bad, bad things." He snags me by the collar and twists, tighter and tighter, roaring, "Take the letter!"

I shout back, "No!" clenching my fists and striking him, once. Then twice. Then again and again — not to inflict pain but to release my anger, my sorrow for this … this bullshit farewell! He doesn't swing back like he said he would or shield himself from my punches, because he knows they'll soon weaken and cease, and shortly, under these darkening clouds, I'll become too distraught, too feeble to fight him any longer.

"It shouldn't've been this way, Udoka. I know."

"Please," I whimper, wheezing. "Just check the ball. I just want one last game, that's it."

"All right. For the letter," he proposes. "I play, you take it." Staring at the pamphlet in his hand, I bow my head warily. Pop folds it into the satchel he brought, while I shuffle my pant leg to my thigh and fasten my knee brace.

As I tie my shoes, I revisit how he used to thread my laces through the holes of a brand-new pair and tie them snug when I was too little to make my own knot. Or, when I aged a bit, how he'd teach me to tighten them from bottom-up so I wouldn't bust an ankle on the court. He *did* care. He always did, deeply. I wouldn't doubt he still does. And actually, he must've sacrificed a lot to let me shoot a pebble-skinned ball at a hoop all my life, perhaps leaving him no other choice but flee to wherever he's going. For whatever reason.

"Your shoestrings," says Pop. "They're dragging on the ground."

"Thanks..."

I stuff the long-looped bunny knots into my socks and adjust my knee brace once more, feeling the first drops of rain hitting my neck.

"Don't mention it."

"No, not that," I say. If this is the last I'll see of him, I might as well get this off my chest: "I don't think I've ever really thanked you for all you've done, with my hoops thing. I guess it took me years to realize and appreciate it all. Thank you for being there at all those games and practices. I'll forever love you for that, Pop."

Pop smiles slightly. He says, "Check," then flips the ball to me and assumes a low stance.

"Yeah. Check."

And so here I am again, amid a shower from the grey sky that quickly soaks my socks and clothes; it slickens the ground and the once-beloved gift given to me right here, years ago. The rain makes Her elusive. I clutch Her a little tighter as I blow by Pop on my two-step gather to the basket, and I'm sure to secure my grip on the ball before I shoot so She doesn't slip away as I let Her go.

Here, I am free.

I'm with Her. I'm with Pop. And in this rain, we're here together — this is my liberation. I'm no longer encaged in my doubts and fears when I dribble and shoot. I'm no longer shackled by the burden of any judgment against my joy to play freely.

This rain, it simply streams down my face as it should. It leaves no hint of the despair that creeps from my eyes and rolls down my cheeks. It gives the ball a slippery feel — the type of slipperiness keeping me from scoring on a lucky bounce or a friendly roll around the cylinder.

To miss a shot seems inevitable in this rain.

But that's all right.

Because I'll no longer worry. I'll no longer fret. My spirit will shine bright and far, whether I make or miss a shot. Because I now know that a shot missed is a shot taken — and that's all that matters.

And I'll live to shoot again.

CHAPTER XXI

WHAT DID YOU DO?

Pop sits across from me by the far edge of the picnic table, dribbling the ball at ankle-height and causing tiny splashes after every bounce. He stares at the thick, smoke-like clouds, wondering for how long they'll ease up, because we're bound to get poured on again at some point. I can't figure out if he's shivering from getting soaked in the storm, or if he's all jittery from the trouble sitting on his mind. But surely, he's unsettled, uneasy. Tense. And I'm beginning to feel the same.

"So, it's true, huh..."

He turns an inch over his shoulder. "What is?"

"That you lose your jumper with all those years of not playing. It's true?"

Terse and bland, still looking into the sky, he goes,

"Guess so."

"And I thought *I* lost it. The rim should've been hula-hoop-sized to keep the score close!"

"Guess it's true." He shuffles to face me. "Guess I lost it."

Glaring into his eyes, I'm hoping they somehow reveal whatever he's been keeping from me. "It's Jame," I question. "Isn't it?"

"Whatcha talkin' 'bout?"

"Jame. Or *Jameis,* his name. Jameis McBendell. The guy all over the news, all over the headlines in the papers. Gone and missing for years. This's about him, the reason you're gonna skip town, isn't it?" I watch Pop bury his face in his hands. "You know him … don't you?"

"I know what he did to you."

"What?"

"No one touches my lil' brother." He grabs me by the wrists, bellowing, "No one!"

I must be blind to the reason he's holding me so tightly, as if he'd nearly lost me.

Then my jaw drops.

That Thursday evening, back in high school. Here, at Woolner Park.

I get a good look at Pop so that he can get a good look at me too, so that he's made aware I'm not messing around when I ask: "What … did you … do?"

Pop hesitates, which only heightens my suspicion. He's definitely hiding something…

"I … I can't get into all that right now," he says, stammering. "Just take the letter!"

"Why?"

"Whaddya mean, '*Why?*'"

"Why should I? Taking it means accepting you leaving."

"That was the deal!"

"Don't you see, Pop? I'm done with ball. Through with it! We can start over, you and me. We can … we can turn the page, make up for lost times right here on these grounds we called Home."

"Too late for that." Pop reaches into his satchel and quickly pulls out the pamphlet, wet with splotches of ink running off the page. "Please. It'll explain some things."

"Know what? Fine … I'll read it." I notice the relief in his brows, his vanishing concerns. "But only if you tell me what happened. *Everything* there is to know."

Thunder shakes the ground, startling the two of us. Pop is frozen in his thoughts.

"Fine," he goes. "Shake on it." He reaches over, and I warily do the same, meeting his palm with mine.

POP'S STORY

I guess I'll start with where I've been all this time. That's the golden question, isn't it: why I've been, y'know, "absent" and all? I bet you've wondered but never once stopped whatever you were doing to ask yourself, "*Hmm, how was Pop dealt such a shitty hand?*"

I was just as good a ballplayer as you were in high school. Maybe even better. You'd spot me somewhere in the sports section of the local paper, every other week — the *Star*, the *Sun*, you name it. I got dozens of letters from several coaches too, who'd each '*loved to have me visit campus for a workout and tour.*'

Come to think of it — hell yeah, I was better than you.

You damn sure know how to get off the ground — I'll give you that. But at my best, I was quicker than you. Stronger than you. A better scorer and playmaker. Tough as nails, and you'd have a slim chance getting by me.

I was gritty. Rough, with a chippy attitude that I used to my advantage. Nothing beat the rush, the high, the pleasure of punishing my opponent, scoring basket after basket and denying him from scoring on me.

See, I was an enforcer. Aggression was my game; aggression was what drove me to the hoop and what drove coaches from down south to come watch me play. Aggression was who I was; it was what made me who I am.

But off the court, I was hotheaded. Combative. Willing to stick my nose into drama that was hardly ever mine. Quick to start a scuffle just being looked at or brushed the wrong way. And it seemed like Jimmy, my right hand and teammate back then, was all for the same deal. Jimmy started the 'Pop' thing. It was cool and all.

The street cred was cool too — *until it wasn't.* Until the day came when we met our match against the wrong people who weren't to be messed with, finding ourselves slumped on a curb in handcuffs.

Blood ran down Jimmy's nose and dribbled onto the pavement. There was a gash splitting his face from his forehead down to his upper lip. As for me, I was shackled at the wrists with regret on my mind. Karma had finally settled the score.

I was booked with a misdemeanour during my senior year for that fight — over something so petty, so stupid! Man, I can't even remember what caused the brawl, but I won't forget how costly it turned out to be.

Word got out to the coaches at all the big-time schools that I was bad news. The recruitment letters dried up, and my chance at going to a good school was gone, which was a tragedy because Ma had been thrilled by the idea of her son heading to college on a full ride. All those years she spent fine-tuning a knucklehead like me into someone who could've been special — they were for nothing.

You were just a bratty little boy, probably whining about whatever when I broke the news to Ma. Leena was the needy preschooler attached to Ma at the hip, if I could remember. But that deathly stare Ma gave me the moment

I confirmed it was all over — I'll never forget it. Your little tantrum and Leena's cry for attention didn't mean a damn thing. I saw my future and Ma's dream vanish as we stood coldly, face to face, eye to eye, for the last time.

Long story short: there's no shiny certificate with my name in print beside the likes of some fancy college. And you wonder why I left? You really wanna know? Blame it on the spite Ma had for me, or the fact that she couldn't find forgiveness or look at me the same. It was either my own guilt or her resentment that I couldn't live with.

So, I left, not knowing when I'd come back. I mean, as you got older, I had to have been there for your games, your camps, your trips to the U.S. But that's about it. Once I learned you were off to prep school, I was like, "Damn! I know he'll be straight!" So I had to let go; I couldn't keep myself tangled in the family madness when I knew you had to focus. The less you knew, the better.

Long story even shorter: *I didn't make it.*

Those four words haunt me, thinking about everything I had going right once upon a time. The news articles, the recruitment letters, the little tastes of glory. They were all gone.

That's why I wanted you to make it, so I could right my wrongs with your accomplishments. Screw that — *our* accomplishments.

Forget "wanted," by the way — screw that too! I *needed* you to make it, you see? When you won, I triumphed with you. When you lost, it felt like I was there too, slouched in a corner of your locker room, all disappointed, wondering, "What if you took *this* shot or made *that* play?"

That's why I was so tough on you all those years. That's why — and I say this without a sorry — I *needed* you to score when you shot the ball. There was no other option. Shoot to score, or don't shoot. Matter of fact, *don't play*. Simple as that.

You had to make it. For me. For Ma. To make things right. Now, do you see?

PRESENT

"That's not enough."

"What's not enough?" asks Pop.

"You can't make this about you! What, just because you told me how you pissed your life away over some silly fight, everything's fine now? You think that makes up for what you put me through?"

"I had my own burdens, my own problems. And you were young. So young. You think I meant to drag you into my mess?"

"Well, you did. And your little story doesn't cut it. Tell me now — what happened to Jame!"

"I'm getting there," Pop replies.

POP'S STORY

I first heard about the stabbing on my way home from the shipping warehouse. I had already been ticked off from a full day of scanning boxes, sealing 'em, and stamping 'em away to the loading crate — which would've been the usual rundown of my workday, but it wasn't, 'cause the floor manager was giving me hell, telling me a customer said her vanity mirror was "cracked when she removed the packaging." I caught the blame since my employee ID matched the box's shipping code, despite the possibility that any package could crack, snap, split, tear, what have you, at any point during delivery (another reason why I was so hard on you with basketball — so you could play for the big bucks and not have to take flak from some asshole about how to pack a friggin' box!).

Anyway, I thought work was the most of my worries that day. The 161 to 35A was my best bet going home, even despite the detour it took, because there were delays with the Line 2 trains that afternoon. One of the stops was by Runnymede Collegiate, and right after, that 35A was full of yappy high schoolers.

I overheard two of them chatting across the aisle: "You hear what happened at the park after school?" one said. "Last Thursday?"

"Old news, homie. A stabbing or something."

I looked over to catch a glimpse. One of them was tall and

slim, squeaky-voiced and fuzzy-haired. Red, fuzzy hair. He had on a short-sleeve button-up and thick reading glasses that kept slipping down his face. The other was a stumpy kid who sported his baseball cap tilted to the side. He had on a tie-dyed shirt that was slitted out down the sleeves.

Leaning closer, I heard the tall one say, "That hotshot ballplayer from Oakwood. He took a slash to the gut, then everyone went bonkers. Nothing too deep, though. Heard he had it coming."

"What's his name again? *Ukuda,* or something?" asked his friend.

"Yeah, something weird like that."

"Shucks, Ukuda. Hate it had to be you."

"'*U-kud-a* told me you were bringing a knife to a ball game!'"

"Ha! '*U-kud-a* tried schoolin' somebody else!'"

"Eh! '*U-kud-a* gave me a warning! *I-kud-a* ran away with a head start!'"

Ukuda this. Ukuda that. It got me heated, fuming! But what really mattered was you getting attacked by some coward like that. I had to cut in.

"You say something 'bout a stabbing? Who did it?" They turned toward me, startled and quiet. But I continued to pry: "He got a name?"

I was about to let my fist rearrange the tall one's jaw when he looked at me and asked, "Who are you?"

But I needed some intel first, so I stormed out of my

seat, grabbed him by his shirt, and pressed my fist into his airway instead. "What is it! The guy's name!"

Wincing, he cried, "Jame! It's Jame!"

"Where is *Jame*?"

"Beats me. He ... he hangs around the park ... Woolner Park ... after school." The kid caught his breath as I eased off his jugular, telling me, "Jame's not the type to be messed with," as if I cared.

They bolted to the rear exit when the bus came to a stop.

PRESENT

I'm beside myself that Pop hasn't realized, or asked, or suspected that his story and how it led us here just doesn't add up. Maybe he doesn't know. Maybe he had to have been there for himself to understand what really went down that night. Or maybe he's in denial. Maybe he *does* know. Maybe he knows he'd acted on sheer impulse and is battling his guilt. Maybe he wants to fess up before he disappears off the face of the Earth. I need to say something.

Pop knocks twice on the table, bringing me back here, drenched and shivering on this bench as though listening to this story at any other time isn't an option. Because really, it isn't — it's either now, or letting my life unfold without knowing the truth. Pop's truth.

"What?" he says worriedly.

"What?"

"You're just sitting there. You gonna say somethin'?"

I must tell him. I gotta tell him. "No … I'm — I'm just lost for words. That's all."

Pop exhales, swaying back and forth to stay warm. "Okay."

I bring my arms in from the sleeves of my hoodie. "T-tell me … what happened n-n-next?"

POP'S STORY

I wound up at Woolner Park, eventually. There must've been something trying to tell me that that day was going to be strange or sinister or just different. And I suppose it had me second-guessing my visit too. I got off the 35A that evening with vengeance on my mind and, from the warehouse, a pair of pliers that I "borrowed."

PRESENT

"You say 'pliers?'"

Pop nods. "I had trouble hiding them under my vest 'cause of how long they were." I gulp, noticing how quiet he's become. "Why'd you ask?"

"No … nothing. Go on."

POP'S STORY

Anyway, I scoped the scene until sundown and waited for any clue, any mention that could point me toward "Jame." I still had time to turn back; violence wasn't me anymore. Then I thought about you and how violence was *never* you, but how you still caught the sharp end of it somehow. So I couldn't turn around.

A fight broke out on the court, but I still had no hint. *Which one was Jame*? I crept closer from the other side of the wire-mesh fence as I heard bodies thudding to the ground. Others swarmed too — except for one. Right away I had an inkling, an intense feeling that the odd man out was the head of all this. *Jame*? Wasn't sure. But I hoped I had just stumbled upon a lead.

A guy broke away from the fistfight and approached this "leader," holding what seemed to have been a comb — but by the way the leader was cowering down, it was surely something sharp. A utility knife, maybe. I thought *he*, the dude with the upper hand, must be Jame.

Someone from the crowd shouted, "Yo, chill out! Put that away!" That someone must've been a teenager — I could hear it in his voice as he dashed toward and stood in front of the guy with the knife.

"Move! Watch out!"

"Jame! Chill!"

I felt goosebumps. Yeah, I heard the name, but from

where? I had to be sure.

"Shut up, Bray!"

Zeroing in on the commotion, I spotted a heavy man in a dark hoodie being held back by this young cat, Bray, who had stood in front of him.

"Nah, Jame! Cut it out!"

There it was. *Jame.* I was so shaken that I mistakenly yanked the fence and blew my cover. I fled the scene remembering those two names — Bray, the tall, peacekeeping youngster, and Jame, my hooded enemy.

Minutes later, I spot the two of them pacing north on Jane, approaching the bushy path leading into the woods of Black Creek. So I trailed them, hanging back in case they turned around and saw me under the streetlights. They split up. Jame took a right into the woods; Bray kept straight on Jane.

So I took a right too.

I'm following this guy, I thought. *I'm doing this. At night, for no one to see.* I coughed on purpose a couple steps behind him, hoping he'd hear me and turn around, confront me or work up some reaction for me to turn away, because I didn't wanna do what I was gonna do.

I coughed again, louder this time, and he still didn't flinch. I realized he was bobbing his head and mumbling to some song.

So I reached into the pocket of my vest, shakily wrapping my fingers around the plier handles. I crept closer, waiting for the right moment. And when it came, I yanked off Jame's hood and tugged him by the shoulder.

The moment was brief, but I got a good look at him.

And what I saw was so frightening and perfectly aligned with the strange and sinister events I had suspected that day.

There was a scar along Jame's face, from the top of his mouth leading to his forehead. I'd seen it before — not as a scar but an open gash.

He looked at me in fright. The pliers fell to the ground, and I stood astounded, realizing that he recognized me. And I recognized him. *Jimmy*.

PRESENT

"So what made you text me to come here?"

"To say goodbye, once and for all. But you gotta make this so hard! If only you'd—"

Instantly I reach out with an open palm, and Pop knows exactly why it's there. He gathers the pamphlet and hands it to me.

I ask Pop, "Why? Why now and not years ago?"

He carefully looks left and right, then leans in before whispering, "They're after me."

"Who is?"

"Who do you think?"

"You … you serious?"

"Think I'd be out here on this cold, damp bench if I wasn't? I woke up this afternoon to someone banging on my front door, having a feeling of exactly who it might've been on the other side. I heard ruffling before they slid a wrinkly cut-out under my door. On it was an old, black-and-white shot of me and Jimmy from high school posing in our team kits. They started interrogating me, asking me if I knew the guy in the picture, where he's at now, what happened at Woolner Park, and so on."

"What … what did you say?"

"I didn't make a single peep. They threatened to break in if I didn't tell 'em what they wanted to know. But when they finally got quiet, I carefully planted my ear to the door. I heard their footsteps disappear into the distance of the hallway."

"Then what'd you do?"

"I packed whatever I could find. I texted you. I grabbed a pen and wrote out my goodbyes on the backside of some pamphlet. Now I'm here. And I gotta go!"

"I … I understand, Pop."

"But before I do…"

He peers at me suspiciously. "What?" I ask him.

"Get up." As I rise, he goes, "Where is it?"

"Where's what?"

"The scar. From the stabbing that those moron kids

were blabbing on about — where is it?" I gulp. "I saw your stomach when you were tussling against me. Your back, your sides too. I took your punches, to my chest and my ribs and my gut. I deserved them. I understood where they came from. But I couldn't understand why there's no sign of you even being *scraped*, let alone shanked, *anywhere*."

He tries tugging at my hoodie, but I don't let him. Instead, I show him myself — my stomach, my back, the sides of my waist — and I see his confusion confirmed. I'm scarless, just like he saw.

"But ... the knife ... who?"

"Not me. I'm sorry."

Pop's trembling in disbelief. "I gotta go," he mutters. Hesitant, he takes me in his arms as though there may not be another chance for an embrace, and that reciprocated feeling — that fear of never seeing someone again — has me cherishing time by the second, hoping that this isn't it for us.

He says, "Don't forget me, brother."

"I won't."

"Don't forget the cherished times. The passion that was sparked the first time you laid your eyes on that thing right there," he says, pointing to the ball in my hands. "That dream of yours, that dream I did all I could to support. Don't forget it — what it meant to you, what I meant to you, who I was to you."

Thunder crashes. Sharp streaks of rain start falling from the sky again. Pop turns toward the storm then hurries onto the street, as the subtle sound of sirens approach. Behind the rainfall, I see flashing colours emerging from the dark. They're blue and red and approaching too.

"C'mon, Pop!" I cry, watching him disappear from the scene. "Pop!"

He's … he's gone.

* * *

Strong winds linger from the storm, leaving my hoodie flailing in the breeze that follows me home. Glancing at the park and the streetlights shimmering on the hoops, I'm shuddering just thinking about what happened to Simeon here, hoping that that nightmare's aftermath is explained in whatever's written on this pamphlet I have on me. I envision what went down by Black Creek years ago, where its trail runs vast with the shrubs and trees surrounding it, where the world saw the last of Jame. Where is he? Is he still alive, or days from now, will I be struck with the shattering news that his body had been found too, dug up with those — I tremble just thinking about them — those pliers?

I'm staring at the screen, typing nervously. There's no turning back if I do this — if I send this off. There's no safe way out of this for me, either. I know too much. On one side, I can't *not* tell her what I was just told. How could I keep that from Mo, and how would I ever be forgiven if she found out that I did? But on the other side, if I do tell her, what happens to Pop? What if he did it? But what if, by the grace of some hole in his story, he wasn't involved in whatever happened to Jame? Because I'm not certain he was; I'm not certain he wasn't.

My thumb hovers over ENTER, but I'm afraid to press it.

The screen goes dim, then blank. My phone dies.

CHAPTER XXII
WEEKS LATER
TALK SOON

Tracing your steps — backtracking to where you've been, what you were doing, what you were thinking — doesn't always explain what you were looking for like you'd hoped it would. And no, I'm not talking about basketball and the blur it's been, at least not this time. I'm talking about the letter Pop gave me weeks back, the one I had promised to read, which should've been tucked inside a pocket of whatever I had on that day. But it wasn't. It wasn't in the hoodie. It wasn't in the sweatpants. It wasn't anywhere in my room. It's still nowhere to be found. I've been up at night ever since, worrying if Pop wrote it vainly, wondering what it would've said. It's gone.

That's why my mind's been stuck on this envelope that Ma's been telling me about since this morning. I rushed out the door with a ball tucked under my arm and some breakfast-to-go in the other hand, catching a word from her before I left. "Good luck! You've got mail, by the way!" she yelled from upstairs.

I wedged my foot in front of the door. "Oh! Where's it, Ma?"

"Kitchen counter, by the spice rack and bananas!"

* * *

So I'm pleased to know it's still where Ma had left it. On the kitchen counter. Right between the revolving spice rack and the not-yet-ripened bananas, just like she said it was, which is a relief, because it puts me at ease knowing at least some things are where they're said to be. It's that peace of mind, that no-surprises feeling keeping me level-headed.

I grab the first butter knife I can find and run it across the seal, lifting the envelope's flap to find the handwritten letter. Leaning against the kitchen counter with my eyes glued to the page, right away I recognize who it's from.

Hey Son,

Sorry for the late response. It seems like there's plenty to write about but nowhere to begin! It's maybe another few hours or so 'til I get back to New Jersey, so I thought now might be a perfect chance to check in with my one and only pen pal. Hopefully I can get to campus sooner than later, because I have a practice to run this evening. Who knows, it could be more of a conditioning session than a practice to get my guys back in shape after a few days off. You know what it's like — there's no time to regress.

I'm glad to see your knee has recovered somewhat well. I mean, somewhat, as in I noticed you were hobbling a bit when I saw you from afar, you and Pierce that is, in the middle of some one-on-one hoops. I guess the rehabbing has been doing some good, since you were out there playing already. Plus it was raining, so you couldn't've been that silly to jump around on wet grounds like that if your knee couldn't take it. I often tell my guys not to mess around playing on solid blacktop, but hey, I guess you know your limits.

Oh, yes. I was there, parked down the street in a rental. That park you were at — not Marie Baldwin, obviously, but the one across from it — Woolner, it's called, right? They've fixed it up quite a bit, haven't they!

Wait, what? Did I read that right?

Your brother had been contacting me quite a bit before then. He must've gotten my info from the coaching staff directory online. It's funny how you and I haven't considered an easier, more efficient, with-the-times method of communicating (I guess because we've been snail-mailing each other ever since your mom and I had split, back when you were far too young to work a telephone or send an email).

Anyway, I saw much more than my sons shooting some rainy-day hoops. Before then, I spotted the two of you bickering like a teenage breakup was going down. I knew I couldn't intervene. It seemed like the wrong time to mess with the distant relationship that you and I share.

Pierce told me a while ago that he screwed up with you, saying he took off during your charity game after seeing you get hurt. He felt terrible leaving you in such pain (knowing that you wouldn't want him seeing you so vulnerable), but he didn't quite know how to break it to you, face to face; he knew he was in for an earful from you whenever you two would see each other next. So he wanted to apologize by having me surprise you with a visit "when the time's right" — his exact words. I guess that's me doing his dirty work, but so be it.

Luckily, I let him know I was already visiting Toronto for that week, schmoozing with the parents of this kid I've been recruiting. Pierce shot me an urgent email, telling me to stop by the Jane and St. Clair area if I could, because he wouldn't've had another chance to make things right with you. And it would've worked out, your surprise party for three, had I skipped traffic and taken main roads, but you and Pierce were already caught up in some dispute by the time I had gotten there, and I couldn't bud in. You can blame that hellish highway for my tardiness — the 401, I believe it was.

In retrospect, I think you and I could agree that my "absence" was best. I was terrified being so near you like that, watching you completely unaware I was around.

A "surprise" would've been too overwhelming for me. I suppose, for you too.

But that wasn't all I saw...

I rest the letter on the countertop, bracing myself. I'm reminded of that afternoon, that pouring afternoon. It's chilling knowing that Pop and I weren't the only ones there.

The two of you had a discussion. A lengthy, heated discussion — which I thought was no longer worth keeping an eye on. But then, you two went your separate ways. You were walking, caught in the wind. Something flew away from whatever you were wearing, and at first, I thought it was nothing — some brochure, a pamphlet, maybe — but as you limped on by, I couldn't help but stare at it drifting down the sidewalk, so I got out of the car and chased it down. And call me a meddler, but the brief window to holler your name and say, "You dropped something!" had closed, and surprising you out of the blue wouldn't've been cool, either.

The pamphlet had "To You" written at the top of it, a strange medium for a formal letter, I'd say. To whom it was intended, I wasn't sure, so I skimmed through it and learned it was Pierce offering you an apology. It's nearly ruined, but I promise to preserve it as well as I can. I'll probably keep it sealed in some jar or something. I gotta give it back to you one day. And I can't wait to hear back from you — I wanna know what that was all about, if that's OK with you.

Back to that rainy day and how surreal it was seeing you

from afar. It made me think of when you were little, around the time I used to visit Canada to scout the talent (there weren't tons of players on my radar during those days, at least from what I can remember — but just like that revamped outdoor court, things have changed tremendously!). Way back then, I couldn't've left for New Jersey without spending some time with you, and I had always longed to see you every offseason, right before the coming training camp, ever since I learned Pierce got you into basketball. I'll always thank him for that, for continuing my legacy with you, even when I wasn't around.

Spotting you at that park years later brought back fond memories. I hope you remember those moments too, despite how young you were. You used to get lost in your own world taking on the Kobes, the LeBrons, hearing my best Marv Albert play-by-play and scoring "buzzer-beating game-winners" on that court. We made it seem real, like you were on TV, playing in front of a sold-out arena. You were a superstar in your own eyes, and I hope that remains. I'll get to that later, though.

Anyway, seeing you in that rainstorm — your growth, your demeanour, your choices of clothing, even watching you play (despite the knee) — was thrilling! It was incredible to witness who you've become. I mean, you had set the bar high the time before then, carrying yourself so well-mannered when I stopped by your high school on St. Clair — but nonetheless, that visit and this recent one both confirmed you are everything I'd expected you to be: a fine young man.

Sorry for showing up unannounced back then, by the way. I went to do some scouting, is all! Oh, that deer-in-headlights look on your old principal's face the moment you realized it was me sitting next to you — she had no clue what was going on! I mean, I was a little surprised too, that you could hardly recognize me, even though I could probably blame how long it's been.

Speaking of me: I'm doing well. You know — coaching at a competitive D-2 program for the past, I'll say, ten — I don't know — dozen-odd years. The pay is stable, and I'm comfortably settled in over here. We should plan something this summer, by the way. Come spend a week or so with your old man! I can give you back Pierce's letter-on-a-pamphlet, too. You could even get a workout in with my guys on campus, if you're still into that! I think it'll be nice.

Anyway, I'll end on this note:

I know I've written this to you before, but I'll write it again: you're no failure, so don't ever think that you are. Don't ever think you weren't good enough. You've wrung out every ounce of basketball in you, and it took courage to do that — to finally look yourself in the mirror and accept that your first, true love is no longer for you. It takes courage to let go.

Let your fate take its course. You'll find who you're destined to be. And it may be tough to accept, but walking away from basketball doesn't make you any less of a person, because one day you'll look back and cherish the journey it took to get you where you are.

Basketball has been a long, long chapter in your life. Be willing to flip the page, even if it seems blank at first. Because soon — this, I promise — you'll find something. Something worth writing about. Something that enthrals your spirit. Something worth living for.

One day, you'll find something real to you again. And when you do, hold on to it with everything you got, and don't let go. Find that purpose. Let it illuminate your soul.

You got this.

Write me back as soon as you can.

Love you, son.

Sincerely,

Your Dad, Clanceton

EPILOGUE

You've been here before. Same game as it's always been; nothing different from the quarterfinal against Carleton, or the championship game at Hoops 'n Hearts, or even the scrimmage in New Jersey the other day. Nothing new. Whether you'll give in to the pressure depends on what you think's at stake. Not what they think, what you think. Don't pay any mind to the score. To the few seconds remaining on the clock. To the people in the crowd on their feet for the final play. They don't matter. None of this should phase you. You know what to do because you've been here before. So, get it done. Do what you gotta do to help the team.

"Simple screen action for Jones! Let's get him free around the foul line! Jones, when you get it, give 'em a jab, then break loose down the lane. If help comes—"

"Make the right play," Jones responds, panting. "Got ... got it."

Jones swipes away the beads of sweat rolling down his chin. He's been torching the defense all afternoon. I mean, he's virtually unguardable today; he's bullied smaller defenders to the basket and zipped past others whose feet were too heavy to stay in front of him.

He's in the zone — that place where everything is clicking exactly how it should click, for you and you only. That place where you feel powerful like never before. That place, that hard-to-find place where anything and everything you do is unstoppable—*the zone*. A place I've longed to revisit.

Until now.

Because I'm in my zone too.

I haven't scored or assisted on a single basket, but I'd be modest to say my impact has been minimal. They need me. There wouldn't be a contest without me.

In the crowd is Leena, sandwiched between a confused Ma and a frantic Mo. Leena gives me her two thumbs up and a grin.

Down the bench, there's Donny and Alex and the others. I can sense the confidence I've instilled in them, this widespread feeling of belief the moment I start talking. Imagine that — confidence. Belief. Passed on from me (me!) to other people. Pop would be proud. Wherever he is.

"I'll be open if they close in on you, Jonesy," says Alex.

"Eh, there's gonna be tons of space around me too," Donny suggests.

"Me too!" adds another.

"Enough, fellas!" I shout, hushing the team. "Let's let Jones make a play. He's got us!"

"All right."

"Yeah!"

"He's right."

Jones hears all the fussing but remains quiet, staring into the frenzied crowd on the opposite sideline. I tap his shoulder slightly and tell him, "No pressure."

His gaze returns to the commotion in the huddle.

Sternly, he responds, "No pressure, Coach."

I'm not convinced, though. On the outside, he's calm and collected. Focused. Level-headed. But I can sense he's nervous. The way he can't seem to make eye contact with me; the fact that he hasn't taken a sip of water during the entire timeout, though I'm nearly certain he's exhausted and really wants one; the feeling that he's here but not really *here* — these are the subtle signs of doubt that only I in this gymnasium can see in this fourteen-year-old phenom who's been a force all game. Little does he know that *I know* all about these uncertain, nervous thoughts racing through his mind; *hell,* I bet I can write a book about what he's thinking right now.

The horn sounds. He gathers himself to hurry onto the court, but not before I tug him by his jersey and speak into his ear.

"Hey, listen up."

Jones nods, fidgety.

"You got this, Jonesy. Be you. Be your best. We need you, man. Don't be hesitant when we need you certain … or, or afraid when we need you brave. This world needs the best that *you* can be. Take your shot, kid … It's your game to win."

He takes a deep breath, looking back at me. And in that instant, I can sense the tension leaving his body.

"Aight, Coach. Got you. I'll do the best I can."

"Not *the* best. *Your* best. Do *your* best and be proud with whatever happens. Have fun out there!"

Jones glances again at the crowd, the referees, the game clock, thumping his fist to his chest. He turns around and says, "Hey, Coach."

"Yeah, Jonesy?"

"Thanks. And … nice pep talk," he says, half-smirking, half-smiling.

I smile back as he hustles onto the hardwood. *Thanks, Jonesy. I thought it was, too. I read it somewhere the other day.*

AUTHOR'S NOTE

I began writing after losing a season-ending playoff game in my third and, as it turned out, final year playing university-level hoops a time when I, bearing my all-time lowest level of confidence, felt empty and confused with basketball. I would soon need to decide whether playing out my upcoming senior year or simply finishing my degree from the sideline was the right move for me. To my plight, committing to either decision was equally as harrowing, troubling, and painful as the other.

I realized I needed an outlet.

I started journaling along my commutes to class, writing aimlessly my feelings, visions, worries, and fears into the "notes" app on my phone (which, believe me, was a cry for help. I had no business logging my feelings anywhere and even used to poke fun at the idea of it). Though eventually, jotting down my thoughts allowed me to reflect in a way that I never felt was possible.

Bullet points turned into paragraphs, and paragraphs into pages. Self-expression became my therapy and storytelling my distraction from the grief of walking away from my first love.

It did take a great deal of courage to produce this story, though; I had speculated that the nature of it could be subject to ridicule, judgement, condescension. Why? Because, throughout my time playing competitive basketball, and especially as perpetuated in the vast realm of sport, confidence (better yet, the lack thereof) is *incredibly* uncomfortable to talk about.

But after deep, deep pondering, I decided to carry on anyway, assuming I hadn't been the only one who had tried shaking free of the burden of self-doubt. I figured if this story could relate to or resonate with someone — *anyone* — then it would fulfill its purpose with the thoughts it'd provoke, the conversations it'd raise.

So, with memories from my playing days, through this novel I feel deeply empowered to challenge a norm that traditionally celebrates stoicism and deplores athletes — specifically, male, teen athletes — for presenting as emotionally vulnerable, "weak," or lacking self-belief. Because from my experiences, the mental toll that comes with playing high-level sports often goes unnoticed, leaving some athletes burdened emotionally, and I wanted to tell that story.

-Jawara

ACKNOWLEDGEMENTS

First and foremost — Dad, thank you for gifting me the game of basketball, along with the countless opportunities, challenges, and lessons that have followed. I'm grateful for the memories, for the good times, and the bad times, too — they've made me who I am.

Thank you, Mom, for supporting me unconditionally, for wanting more for me than I'll ever want for myself. You challenge me to be a better son, a better human being — thank you for that.

Aisha, you've helped me find not only my voice, but more so the courage to share a glimpse of what I've felt in my heart for quite some time. I'm happily indebted to you.

Nat, through your grace and unwavering patience, you've dealt with every side of me throughout the making of this story. Thank you — you're the greatest teammate I've ever had.

Allister — your guidance, editorial support, and advocation for my story will *never* be forgotten. Draft after draft (… *after draft*), you've been there, offering invaluable advice throughout this wild, unpredictable process. I can willingly admit that *The Hoop and the*

Harm might've been laughably impossible without you!

To the fine folks at Lorimer, I'm truly grateful for the opportunity to share a story that I felt needed to be told. Thank you sincerely for this publication, for challenging me to bring this novel to its peak potential.

To Antonio Michael, Cabbie, Tychon, and Drew: I'm grateful to have crossed paths with each of you. Thank you all for your support of my story.

Ms. Carinci and Mr. McInnis — I'm deeply grateful to have had you both in my life throughout my most youthful, impressionable years. Thank you for instilling such fundamental values in me — I carry many of your lessons with me to this day. Somewhere, there *should* be a private school or gymnasium named after you two — if you ask me, at least!

To my former teammates and coaches, my friends and peers with whom I've shared an open gym, thank you for being a part of my journey.